ONCE UPON
A WISH

DANYELLE FERGUSON

ONCE UPON
A WISH

DANYELLE FERGUSON

WONDERSTRUCK BOOKS

Published by Wonderstruck Books, Kansas City, KS
ISBN: 9780998088631
Cover design by Steven Novak
Cover design © 2017 by Wonderstruck Books
Interior design by Wonderstruck Books

DEDICATION

This one's for you, Lisa Swinton! Movie nights, chocolate, and long distance conversations are the foundation of our friendship. Thanks for keeping me sane. You are the bomb!

CHAPTER ONE

Monday, September 18th

DELPHINE TAPPED HER FOUNTAIN PEN against the notebook lying open on the café table. The blank pages defiantly glared at her, daring her to jot down ideas for her next novel. Instead she dropped the pen and slouched back into the metal chair, readjusting her position to match her pout. Except the stupid, straight-backed chair wasn't cooperating, so she shifted into a more lady-like position and crossed her legs before reaching for her drink.

The china demitasse cup rattled against its saucer as she hastily picked it up to calm her frustration with some *chocolat chaud*. The hot cocoa was like sipping liquid decadence. Creamy milk and rich dark chocolate melted into a velvety indulgence that made her taste buds burst with delight. A stark contrast to her first trip abroad as a young girl, when she was introduced to instant hot cocoa. Delphine felt bad for the poor Americans who came to her country, experienced this *magnifique* concoction, then had to return to their country's poor watery substitute.

Hugo, her Yorkie Terrier, whined at her feet. She set the cocoa aside, then motioned for him to jump onto her lap, where he snuggled in. She had hoped that escaping her cramped apartment to sit at her favorite café across from La Rochelle's stone towers and soak in the autumn's salty ocean breeze would rejuvenate her creative brain. Instead, the pressure of writer's block and a looming deadline weighed on her.

Her first three novels had received great reviews, fairly good sales, and a solid readership. It was her fourth novel that had shocked her by hitting several bestseller lists. Now, instead of her editor kindly inquiring about her next project, Michel was pushing for updates to pass onto the publisher's buying committee.

The combination of stress to produce another bestselling book and the fear of letting her readers down had sucked all the creativity out of her.

What if four novels was all she had in her? What if she was a one-time bestselling wonder?

She wished she could talk to her favorite brainstorming partner, but Maman was currently out of commission and would be, well, for a long time. No, Delphine was on her own for this one. She took a deep breath to calm the quick flutter of her heart.

"What do you think, Hugo? Should we give up for the day?" Hugo's nose twitched and he sneezed, then shook his head back and forth to clear away whatever had tickled his nose. Delphine laughed. "I'll take that as a sign we should stick it out a while longer." She continued to pet him, the motion soothing both of them.

She shifted her gaze to the cobblestone-paved plaza, hoping the mundaneness of everyday life would inspire her. There were the usual tourists, making their way from tours at Maison de Henri II into the port to snap photos of the majestic entry towers and multi-colored sail boats lining the ocean front. Teenagers from the local *lycée* school made their way to various vendors for a pastry before heading home or to the bus depot. She spotted a few university students sitting on ledges, ear buds in place as they studied their electronic tablets. Delphine's lips lifted into a smile as she spied mothers chatting as their children scrambled around the plaza fountain, playing a game of tag. A child darted through a group of young men, causing one of them to stumble backward, arms flailing before regaining his balance.

"*Pardon, monsieur,*" another child yelled as they continued the chase.

The man who stumbled simply waved them on as his friends patted his back and teased him about the incident. The mothers, though, called their children back to them, clearly correcting their rambunctious behavior before gathering their things together to leave. One little girl tugged on her mother's shirt to capture her attention before pointing to the fountain where a group of teenagers had stopped to toss coins in. The mother responded with a firm shake of her head. The child grabbed her younger sibling's hand and cast a longing glance at the wishing fountain before disappearing with her family down another street.

Delphine loved the fountain's classic pedestal design and the ornate flowers carved into the side, each unique and intricately detailed. The water bubbled up from the center and filled the pedestal's bath before gracefully landing in the pool below.

4

The teens who cast in their coins had their heads together, whispering and giggling before moving on. Delphine couldn't remember the last time she believed in the whimsy of wishing fountains. She certainly had before her family moved from France to Switzerland in her tween years, forcing her to leave her friends behind. Now, with her adult perspective, she was grateful for those bitter months during her formative years. It was then that her love of reading morphed into a passion for creating stories, the characters becoming her friends, her lifeline to surviving a foreign country.

Maybe what she needed was to recapture some of her youthful whimsy. After all, if she was writing for teens, she should try to get into their perspective a little more. Delphine pulled out her change purse and used a finger to push the coins around until she found the one she was looking for. She clicked her tongue to get Hugo's attention. After a hand signal, he leapt from her lap and settled in the shade under the café table.

Thank goodness for those obedience school classes, she thought as she tied his leash to her chair. While dogs could go just about anywhere with their owners in France, they were expected to be well-behaved. She tested the leash's knot, then signaled for Hugo to stay where he was.

With the coin pressed firmly into the palm of her hand, she crossed the short distance to the fountain. She skirted away from a few groups until she found a little isolated spot that seemed just right. She opened her fingers and nudged the coin with her thumb, wondering what to wish for.

As a child, she often wished for an ice cream treat or to visit her Aunt Valérie's so she could go horseback riding. Teenagers probably spent most of their wishes asking for the attention of a certain special someone. Not that romance was unappealing, but Delphine preferred the predictability of her character's love stories. No matter how much conflict they endured, they always ended up together.

Real-life relationships didn't come with that guarantee, and Delphine found that terrifying. Her wants these days had more to do with hoping for a royalty check big enough to pay the bills, buy groceries, and have enough left over for something fun. Those checks weren't going to keep coming if she didn't produce another book. So she ditched fanciful and went for practical. She

6

closed her eyes and squeezed the coin.

All I wish for are story ideas. Well, not just any story idea, a magnifique Sci-Fi YA story, one that my readers will love. Because no matter what the sales numbers turn out to be, having happy readers is the ultimate goal.

Delphine took a deep breath and sent her wish out into the universe before she opened her eyes and tossed the coin into the fountain. Her gaze followed its path through the air, but she was shocked when another coin collided with it before they both hit the water with a big plop and sank.

She gasped, then looked around to find a man whose face reflected a similar feeling of surprise.

He was handsome in a preppy casual sort of way. Jeans were paired with a white dress shirt, topped with a deep green v-neck sweater, both sets of sleeves pushed up to his elbows. His hairstyle completed the look, the dark waves giving it a tousled, careless vibe. What would it feel like to sink her fingers into his hair? Would it feel as silky as it looked? Or would she be disappointed to find it sticky with hair product?

Her heart fluttered again, not from anxiety, but from the hesitant smile that appeared on his face. He lifted his hand in a wave. Delphine tried to swallow past the lump forming in her throat, but her mouth had gone dry. Her hand inched up, ready to return his greeting, but what if—*gasp!*

What if she had a set of characters who were crushing on each other, but just when they were finally brave enough to admit their feelings, they were forced apart? But why? It would need to be something against their will, something they couldn't control but absolutely had to follow.

Delphine's hand dropped back to her side. She knew well the tragedy of leaving friends behind, but what would it be like to abandon your newly discovered true love?

She dashed back to the café table. Hugo greeted her with a little yip before settling back down, his front paws and head lying across one of her feet. She flipped the notebook open and uncapped her fountain pen. As soon as the nib hit the paper, details about the two main characters flowed. It wasn't the most original idea; in fact, it had been done before, many times over, but this time, it was her story, and that made it unique.

Delphine didn't know how to describe the story unfolding in her mind. Tidbits about the characters turned into fully fleshed beings: their likes, dislikes, characteristics, scraps of dialogue, how they reacted to their feelings being crushed. As those details came together, so did conflicting ideas for the setting and the culture's background. Delphine flipped forward several pages in the notebook, bent a corner, then jotted down those notes to review later before flipping back to the character section. She didn't even mind sipping the cooled *chocolat chaud* as she became even more absorbed in Candessa and Felix's story. *Yes, Candessa and Felix*, she thought, nodding and adding their names at the top of their bio pages. The characters were blooming and coming to life right before her.

Discovery was her favorite part of the writing process. When the passion of creation flowed through an author, it was the headiest drug, addicting in its own perfect way. It was like having a front row seat to witnessing the majesty of God creating the heavens and the earth. If she pursued that flow, if she heeded the promptings of her muse, then the results would be a marvelously beautiful thing.

CHAPTER TWO

EVERYTHING AROUND JEAN-PAUL seemed to be changing, like there was an electric charge in the air. It all started when he discovered that beat up coin next to the fountain. He almost passed it by, but instead dislodged it from where it was wedged between a cobblestone and the fountain. It was an old French franc. Now that euros were the accepted form of currency, the former French currency had either been turned into banks to be exchanged for euros or hidden away hoping that one day the francs would be rare enough to make a coin collection more valuable.

Jean-Paul turned the coin around, examining both sides. What journey had led the coin to this particular place? As a child, his grandmother always said it was bad luck to toss a coin into a fountain without making a wish first. So before he could discard it, the coin needed a proper wish. His grandma also said the best wish a coin could receive involved a request for love. Jean-Paul shrugged and dismissed that idea. Relationships always ended with a crash-and-burn nose-dive at the end. The coin would just have to settle for what he really wanted—more clients for his marketing firm.

He had recently opened a new branch of his father's marketing firm in La Rochelle, focusing specifically on online and social marketing. So far he had added a few new clients on top of his father's existing clientele. If only he could get the right network connections within the nautical or tourism communities, then he could make some leeway in growing the business.

Not that he lacked opportunities. Their long-time friends and business associates, the St. Germain family, had made it their mission to introduce him to all their friends, one tedious social event after another. At first it all seemed innocent enough, but lately, the outings centered around escorting their daughter, Angelique, to various events that were more centered on appearing in the society columns than actually making business connections.

He liked Angelique well enough. After all, they'd known each other for their entire lives, even spending at least one family vacation together each year. But these days it was rare to catch a glimpse of the friend he grew up with. Somehow between their university years and now, in their late twenties, she had changed from a young woman with convictions and a strong vision for her future to a society diva, with the matching wardrobe and personality. On top of that, he had picked up on some clues indicating the hopeful expectation for their friendship to evolve into something, well, more than what his heart felt.

Which brought him back to his biggest priority at this particular time of his life— his work.

I wish for the opportunity to get into the right networks so I can expand my father's marketing company.

With the flick of his thumb, he sent the coin flying through the air. He almost turned away rather than watching it. After all, he had seen dozens of coins plop in fountains, but something kept him rooted to that spot. His eyes followed the path of the coin, leading right to the beautiful woman tossing in her coin from the other side. He barely saw the two coins' collision. He really didn't care about them. It was the hopeful look on her face that drew his attention. Then the round 'oh' of her mouth when her expression turned to surprise. He felt like he was in *lycée* again, raising his hand to wave to the pretty girl he was too shy to greet.

His heart plummeted when she dashed away, but the look of inspiration on her face was unforgettable. Her destination ended up being a café table she had obviously occupied before their moment at the fountain. He had no idea what she was writing, but it filled her with passion. There was no other word that better described her complete preoccupation with her project. It was mesmerizing.

When was the last time he felt so strongly about a project that the rest of the world melted away?

He checked the schedule on his calendar, and even though the timing would be a bit tight, he decided to set up his work at a table on the other side of the café. Once the laptop was set up, Jean-Paul tried to get some website design done, but his progress slowed every time he glanced up at the young woman. He smiled as she pushed her long sandy blonde curls away from her face yet again, knowing in a few moments the wind would pick them up and blow them back.

What was she doing that was so fascinating?

Beep, beep.

He picked up his cell phone to check the caller ID. Seeing it was the secretary for Monsieur St. Germain, he answered. "*Bonjour*, Madame, how are you?"

"Wonderful, Jean-Paul," Madame Wiedmaier replied. "Monsieur St. Germain would like to set up an appointment to discuss Simply Bella's upcoming holiday promotions and schedule of website updates."

"*Absolument.*" He pulled up the calendar on his laptop.

Across the café, the woman picked up her demitasse cup, took a sip, then wrinkled her nose before quickly replacing it and nudging it away from her work. Jean-Paul smiled and signaled for the waitress.

"Would next week on Monday afternoon work?" he asked Madame Wiedmaier.

"*Parfait*," she responded. They exchanged a few more details, then ended the call.

Jean-Paul turned his attention to the

14

waitress, whose name tag displayed her name as Fleurette. "*Merci* for waiting. I would like to order a refill for the mademoiselle at the table there," he said, motioning toward the mysterious woman.

"Oh, *oui*, monsieur. She is having *chocolat chaud*. I can relay a message as well, if you'd like." Fleurette's eyes radiated delight with the task given her.

Without hesitation, Jean-Paul said, "Tell her I hope her wish was granted."

Fleurette nodded and left to fulfill the order. As soon as she disappeared, Jean-Paul realized just how idiotic his message sounded. Why didn't he simply inquire if he could join her?

His face flushed with heat as he anxiously typed up some notes for his meeting with Monsieur St. Germain, dreading the moment when the *chocolat chaud* would be delivered. Then Fleurette left the café with a demitasse and saucer, heading straight for the woman's table. He didn't want to watch, but he couldn't force his eyes away. His heart pounded. This was worse than watching a horror show and knowing the person in the shower was going to be killed. This was happening right now. Not on a big screen but in his very own real-time.

Fleurette greeted the woman, then set the cup and saucer down. The woman's eyes widened before they darted to him. He tried to smile, but he probably looked like a moron. She bit her lip as Fleurette delivered his message before lowering her head and muttering something to the waitress, who winked at him as she made her way back into the café.

What should he do next? Go to her table and introduce himself? Pack up and leave? He did have a meeting in twenty minutes back at his office, so his time was running short. He didn't want to leave without at least meeting her. The indecision was killing him. He was about to close his laptop when he saw Fleurette return with another demitasse and saucer, which she also placed at the woman's table.

Who was the second cup for? The woman closed her journal and chewed on her bottom lip for a second before releasing it. His heart pounded, waiting to see what her next move would be. Then she made eye contact with him and motioned to the seat across from her.

Zut alors! Jean-Paul quickly gathered his stuff, then crossed to her table. He let his bag swing off his shoulder to rest beside the chair before extending his hand.

"*Bonjour*, mademoiselle. I'm Jean-Paul Chassériau."

His fingers enveloped her tiny hand, but she returned the handshake with a firm grip. Small but confident. He liked that.

"My name is Delphine."

It was odd she didn't give her last name, but perhaps she was just being cautious. Smart since she was meeting someone new. Her small dog yipped from under the table, and Delphine patted her knees. A scruffy ball of fur leapt up, then sat on her lap. Her dog was more black than the typical brown and white the Yorkie breed was known for, giving him a tough scrapper look despite his small size.

"And this is Hugo, my ferocious guard dog. Say hello, Hugo." The Yorkie tilted his head as if considering Jean-Paul, then lifted his paw to obey.

Jean-Paul took the tiny paw in his hand and shook it. "Very nice to meet you," he said in a deep, serious voice. When he released Hugo's paw, the dog's tongue darted out and licked the side of Jean-Paul's thumb.

"He likes you," Delphine said, petting her dog.

He took her comment as a good thing and sat down in his chair.

"So, did I ruin your wish?" she asked.

Jean-Paul smiled. She liked to jump right to the point, no tiptoeing around. "No, not at all. I've never seen two coins collide like that."

"Ah, but just because you haven't seen it, doesn't mean it hasn't happened. Statistically, anyway," Delphine said, picking up the cup and saucer.

"I'm willing to admit the probability is non-zero, but I can't imagine it would be very high," Jean-Paul shot back, interested to see her response to his geeky comment.

"Tell me," Delphine said, leaning forward, intrigue glinting in her eyes. "How many coins have you seen thrown into that fountain?"

He folded his arms and brought up one finger to tap his chin, going for a deep-in-thought pose. "You're right. Maybe we should perform an experiment. How about we meet here again on Thursday?"

His pulse sped up, wondering if she'd accept his invitation.

Beep beep.

Dang it all. He pulled out his cell phone and grimaced when he saw the time. "I'm sorry, just one minute." He pressed the button to answer. "*Bonjour*, Helena." He paused, listening as his secretary informed

18

him that his client had arrived early. "*Oui*, I am on my way now and should be there in about ten minutes. *Merci*." He ended the call, sad to see his meeting with Delphine end. "My client arrived early for an appointment, so I need to leave. I'll be here Thursday afternoon about three o'clock. Perhaps you'll join me." He pulled out a business card from his tote and handed it to her. "In case you'd like to contact me."

She took the card, tapping it against the palm of her hand. "Perhaps."

He slung the strap of his tote over his shoulder, ready to hurry to his office.

"Oh, Jean-Paul," she said, pulling him to a halt before he dashed off. "Be sure to bring extra coins for the experiment."

A jolt of pleasure rushed through him as he nodded. "*Absolument*," he said just before parting ways.

When he turned onto the street where his office was located, he pulled out his cell phone and blocked out the time on Thursday so his secretary wouldn't schedule any conflicting appointments. This was one meeting he would be sure not to miss.

CHAPTER THREE

Thursday, September 21st

DELPHINE RAISED HER ARMS for a deep stretch and yawned, then pushed her chair back. She needed to walk away from the manuscript for awhile before her brain turned into a shriveled tangerine. Plus, it was never a good sign when her tush went numb from sitting for so long.

Over the last three days, she had stayed holed up in her apartment and written almost twenty-three thousand words on the new novel, which she tentatively titled *Two Worlds Apart*. She stank at coming up with book names. Thankfully her editor did an excellent job of correcting that weakness.

Her word count should have made her happy. Normally it meant she was about one-third of the way through. This time, though, she had a feeling a lot of those words would go into the Deleted Scenes folder. While she had a strong vision for the characters and their conflict, she was still hung up on how they were actually going to be separated.

If only she could talk with Maman. What Papa had hoped was mild memory loss had been diagnosed as Alzheimer's the previous month. The nasty disease was taking hold of her mother's memories and erasing them little bit by little bit. She was already confusing Delphine for a younger version of her Aunt Valérie. At least Maman remembered Papa. For now.

Delphine pushed the worry and fear of the future deep down, afraid that if she lingered too long, she would turn into a puddle of mushy tears. Instead she refocused on the present. It was Thursday, and she was meeting Jean-Paul soon.

But first, a girl needs some sustenance, she thought, putting a hand over her rumbling stomach. She prepared a late lunch of salad, baked Brie, and a homemade vinaigrette. Once the meal was cleaned up, she retreated to her bedroom to change for her date with Jean-Paul. But was it an official date? She mulled the question over as she exchanged her pajama bottoms for a pair of jeans, then pulled a fitted black shirt over her head.

After all, they hardly knew each other. So that made today's meeting the zeroth date, she decided. The date before the first date. They were conducting a relationship experiment, first to satisfy their curiosity about each other, and second to see if there was a spark that would lead to a first date or if it would all end with a disappointing false start.

She retrieved her favorite heather-gray knit cardigan from a drawer, then threaded her arms through it. Of course, there was a third possible scenario. What if one of them ended up liking the other, while the other person wasn't feeling the warm glow of affection, which led to confusion, awkwardness, and future social avoidance? And what if the person who was feeling the love continued to try to attract the person who wasn't? That would be worse than crashing like a rocket that didn't achieve maximum escape velocity.

Delphine rubbed her forehead where an ache was beginning to throb. Did she really want to go on this non-date? There were so many other things she could be doing: restocking her cabinets with food, giving Hugo his weekly bath, or surfing the web for inspiration for her manuscript.

Stop it, Delphine. We are doing this. Jean-

Paul was witty and intriguing and yes, attractive. Get your tush out of over-analytical mode and focus on your next step. She twisted open the cap of her lip gloss, then rolled the fruity concoction across her lips.

"One final touch," she said, draping a long silver chain around her neck. She pivoted, checking her appearance from a variety of angles. "All ready."

She grabbed a hand bag next to the front door. "Hugo," she called out. "*Allez!*"

A yip sounded from the living room as he jumped from the couch and came running, excited to escape the apartment for a walk. She clipped a leash to his collar, then locked her apartment door and they were off.

Delphine followed the cobblestone road toward the plaza, greeting some of the neighborhood *grandmères* who sat on chairs near their front doors, gossiping and soaking up the autumn sunshine. After a few blocks, the cobblestone street opened up to the plaza. She paused, her heart fluttering at the sight of the wishing fountain in the center of everything. She checked her watch, noting that she was a few minutes early. Would Jean-Paul be here already? Hugo hopped up, putting his paws on her leg.

"You're the only one I'm going to admit

23

this too, Hugo, but I feel like a bottle of Coca-Cola is going to explode in my tummy." Hugo rubbed his snout on her leg, offering his own brand of encouragement. She gave his head one last pat before taking a deep breath. "Let's do this."

She took a confident step forward, only to have the heel of her boot slip on the cobblestones. She pitched forward and stumbled before regaining her balance. Laughing to ease the embarrassment swelling inside, she quickly looked around, hoping no one noticed her less-than-graceful moves. Thankfully, they all seemed preoccupied with their own lives rather than looking her way. She continued into the plaza, eventually spotting Jean-Paul leaning casually near the café entrance.

Ooh là là! The man looked just as wonderful as she remembered. His hair still had that sexy tousled look that made her itch to sink her fingers into it. This time his dress shirt was white with dark stripes, topped with a black v-neck sweater and paired with corduroy pants. Everything seemed tailored to fit his athletic physique just right. Why was he interested in her—the girl who was the complete opposite? Her fashion style was all about simplicity and comfort, while his was straight out of GQ.

"*Bonjour*," Jean-Paul called, waving to capture her attention.

She returned his smile and greeting as she led Hugo toward him. "*Bonjour*, Jean-Paul," she responded, reciprocating a *bise* kiss on the cheek.

"And how is your ferocious guard dog today?"

She was delighted when he knelt beside her to say hello to Hugo. The little imp playing coy, raising his paw for a handshake. Jean-Paul looked up, his blue eyes reflecting happiness and contentment. How did anyone find the strength to look away after discovering how captivating they were? She blinked, realized she missed something he said, and tried to refocus. "I'm sorry, I didn't quite hear you."

He straightened and pulled a small bag of euro coins out of his pocket. "I said I came prepared. Shall we test our experiment?"

Oh yes, the fountain. She quirked her eyebrow. "How do you propose we go about it?"

"I thought we could start by taking up our original locations." Jean-Paul gestured for her to lead the way toward their destination.

They paused to distribute the coins

before separating. Delphine cupped her hands together, waiting for her portion. His hand brushed against hers as he counted out ten coins. Her heart leapt, and tingles spread through her from such a simple touch. She clenched the coins in her hand, trying to quell the unexpected feelings. The science geek in her wondered if it was an anomaly or something unique to Jean-Paul.

Thankfully, he didn't give her time to dwell on it. They each returned to their wishing spots from the other day. "What now?" she called across the fountain.

"I thought for the first three tosses, we could close our eyes, then count down and toss the coins as soon as we opened our eyes. No aiming."

She nodded her agreement and closed her eyes. Memories of that day at the fountain rushed back to her. The children at play, the giggly teenagers. Her wish . . . Was meeting Jean-Paul part of the fountain's answer for her?

"*Un . . . deux . . . trois . . .*" Jean-Paul counted, bringing her back to the present.

She both opened her eyes and tossed. Delphine's coin traveled closer to the center of the fountain while Jean-Paul's went the opposite direction. They laughed, then tried two more times, each taking turns counting down before the toss, but without any successful collisions.

"How about if we try to aim our coins at each other?" Delphine suggested. The next three tosses were much closer, as they strategized and did their best to line up their coins. One set missed each other by mere centimeters.

"Apparently our aim is faulty. It's a good thing we aren't pitchers for a sporting team," she said. Pleasure swelled inside as Jean-Paul chuckled at her remark. "What shall we attempt next?"

Jean-Paul transferred the coins back and forth between his hands. "How about we throw them all at the same time?" At her nod, he counted down. "Ready. *Un, deux, trois!*"

Two sets of four coins arced through the air toward each other. Delphine was sure that this time at least one coin would bump into another. Instead, each completed its journey with eight distinct uninterrupted plops into the water. She lifted her hands in defeat, then Jean-Paul jogged around the fountain to where she waited.

"So, what's your conclusion?" he asked.

"Hmm." She tapped one finger against her chin, considering her hypothesis and the actual outcomes. "Obviously we failed to get the results we hoped for, but why? Was it that we needed more coins? Or perhaps the position of the moon and sun has changed the gravitational pull and we need to shift our positions? My opinion is that the results are inconclusive. *Et tu?*"

"I concede those are all good points. Perhaps more experiments and data are needed to achieve success. Or . . ." Jean-Paul paused, shoving his hands in his pockets and rocking back on his heels.

"Or?" she said, prompting him to continue. His smile made the corners of his eyes crinkle, adding a touch of merriment to the sincerity she saw in the blue depths.

"Or perhaps our coins colliding was the universe's way of introducing us to each other."

Warmth suffused her cheeks and she ducked her head, breaking their eye contact. She twisted Hugo's leash around her hand, pleased with Jean-Paul's flirting, but her innate shyness made her worry if she said anything, she'd babble or stammer all over herself.

"Or maybe I'm just corny," Jean-Paul countered with a shrug of his shoulders, trying to fill the short gap of silence.

She bit her lip, then peeked up at him. *Be brave*, she told herself. "I can see the merit of your conclusion. Um, not the corny conclusion. The first one." Her blush kicked up a few notches, but the resulting smile that appeared on his face was worth it.

"I heard the weekly flea market is today. Would you like to explore it with me?" Jean-Paul asked.

She nodded. "I have to warn you, though, Hugo loves to show off for the vendors."

"Then that will make it all the more interesting," he said, gesturing toward the direction of the market.

Side-by-side, they left the plaza behind for the bright colors and various products of the Place de la Motte Rouge flea market. Pottery, clothing, funky old lamps, used books, and refurbished furniture were just a sampling of the items on display.

"What brought you to La Rochelle?" Delphine asked as they sorted through some boxes of vinyl records while Hugo rested in the shade under the table.

"Work. My family owns a marketing firm in Nantes. Dad's very traditional—print, billboards, mailers, and the like. He has a solid clientele in Nantes, but I wanted to branch out." He paused, pulling out a recording of Michael Jackson's Thriller album. "Do you remember this?"

"That music video used to give me nightmares." Delphine shivered, remembering the sluggish feel of her legs barely moving while the zombies with glowing eyes got closer and closer. "Now this is more my style." She held up another classic.

"No," Jean-Paul said, making a cross with his fingers to shield himself.

"But girls just wanna have fun." Delphine winked and slid the Cyndi Lauper record back into place. "So why La Rochelle?"

Jean-Paul gestured to the flea market. "Look at this place. It's Thursday afternoon, yet the flea market is filled with college students and young parents. I'd say the median age is probably twenty-eight. Pretty soon the teenagers will be joining the mix. La Rochelle has a fascinating blend of history, youthful energy, and hip technology. It's perfect for our new branch."

"*Allez*, Hugo," she commanded as they moved to the next booth, this one hosting an assortment of recycled sculptures made from household items like utensils and light bulbs. "Tell me more," Delphine said, continuing the conversation.

Jean-Paul lifted an eyebrow. "You sure? I don't want to bore you before I can

30

convince you to go on an official date."

She playfully bumped her shoulder against his, feeling as if butterflies were swarming inside from his allusion to another date. "Yes, I'm intrigued."

"So, I grew up working at my Dad's office, right? And I learned a lot about solid marketing. At the same time, as a young teen, I saw social media really gain traction. With all the advancements in technology, our generation and younger aren't turning to magazines or newspapers for information on what to buy. They're clicking on social media ads, using the Internet to search for the best reviews, deals, or coupon codes. Just about everything they want can be accessed from the phone in their pockets. It's all about creating websites that aren't stagnate, but engage their target market and pull them into social media interaction. That's the side of marketing I love."

She was utterly fascinated. Here was a man who knew his niche and embraced it. His enthusiasm was expressed through his words, but also showed through his hand movements as he talked and the way the tone of his voice changed. It was lighter, flowing smoothly and confidently.

"Sorry if I'm going on too much." He stumbled to a stop.

She placed her hand on his arm. "No, I enjoy your enthusiasm. It's just the people-watcher in me that is soaking it all in. Can you show me some of your work?"

Jean-Paul pulled out his phone, swiping and clicking on a few things before showing her the screen. "Today I was working on redesigning a company's logo to make it more festive for the upcoming holidays."

She recognized the vintage store's brand and admired the way he took the classic design and added touches of holly berries and pine branches to add a seasonal look without overwhelming the original logo. "It's *fantastique*."

"*Merci*," he said before stowing away the phone and turning his full attention to her. "What about you? I was fascinated by whatever you were working on the other day."

"I'm a writer, actually. A story idea had just popped into my head, and I was getting it all down in my notebook."

They moved toward the next vendor, but Hugo saw one of his favorite stops up head. Le Bon Chien. He yipped and tugged at the leash.

"Let's hold that thought for a moment," Delphine suggested as they changed course and let Hugo take the lead.

The pudgy bald man bent down to greet his guest. Hugo sat obediently, although they could see his excitement as his little body shook. "Ah, *bonjour, mon ami* Hugo. How are you today?"

"Monsieur Ledoux ran the obedience school we attended," Delphine explained. Jean-Paul nodded, and they both watched as Hugo obeyed his teacher's various commands, each time receiving a small treat as a reward.

"*C'est bon*," Monsieur Ledoux said, satisfied with Hugo's performance. He selected a small bag of treats and gave them to Delphine for safekeeping. Another family arrived with a mischievous puppy, cutting their visit short.

"Quite proud of himself, isn't he?" Jean-Paul motioned to Hugo's new swagger.

Delphine looped the leash over her wrist. "Ah, yes, Monsieur Ledoux has that effect on him. I sometimes imagine that Hugo believes he is the prince and our lives circle around him."

Jean-Paul tilted his head as he regarded Hugo. "From his perspective, it could be entirely true. He gets to nap when he wants, doesn't make any of his own food, and even gets lots of love from his owner too. The life of a pet can be rather indulgent. Although, I don't think Hugo should be the only one who gets spoiled. How about a treat for us?"

They chose a vendor selling hand-dipped ice cream. After they both had double scoops—chocolate for her, strawberry for him—they found a bench to sit on. Hugo circled around, then curled up between their two sets of feet.

"So what do you write? I'm going to feel really stupid if you tell me you write for a magazine."

Laughter bubbled up. She hadn't even thought of that when she disclosed she was a writer. "That would have been just too perfect for torture. *Non*, I write novels for teenagers. Generally something with a science fiction or speculative twist."

His eyebrows scrunched together as he licked at his ice cream. Then he asked, "I know what science fiction is, but what makes a book speculative? Is that like a mystery?"

"I get that question a lot." She enjoyed some of the chocolate yumminess before it dripped down the cone, then continued. "There are so many terms we use in the publishing industry that don't always cross over to readership and book stores. Speculative fiction is one of the more complicated genres, in my opinion. It covers a wide range of elements. It can be futuristic like *Ender's Game*. Sometimes it has a contemporary setting with a supernatural element like *The Hourglass Door* series. It can even be a broken world or have a dystopian feel like the *Hunger Games* series. Did any of that help?"

Jean-Paul still looked slightly confused. "So where does Harry Potter fit in?"

"Ooh," she said. "Now that's controversial. Some say it's fantasy, others classify it as speculative. Let me give you a tip," she said, leaning forward and dropping her voice to a conspiratorial whisper. "If you're ever in a group of die-hard fans, don't bring up that topic or you may end up crushed at the bottom of a stampede."

He made a little check-mark action in the air. "Duly noted. HP is off limits."

She smiled at his sense of humor. At the beginning, she had been nervous, but it only took a few moments before the fizzy anxious feeling had settled. The rest of their time together had been filled with ease, good conversation, and a growing curiosity about the spark of attraction she felt between them.

Jean-Paul twisted his ice cream cone around, catching a drip on the other side. The cone was dwarfed by his two very well made, strong hands. Hands that made her tingle and her heartbeat quicken.

Delphine blinked to clear her thoughts. Earlier it was his eyes, now his hands. She seriously had to stop thinking things like that. It was all starting to sound like a cheesy romance novel. She hated cheesy romance novels. Real life just wasn't like that . . . Was it?

"I have to be honest," Jean-Paul said, shifting his position on the bench to face her better. "Even though I noticed you at the fountain, it was when you dashed back to the table and were totally absorbed in your story that I knew I needed to meet you. Your passion and focus intrigued me. It makes sense now that I know you're a writer. Creative people tend to be more caught up in their work."

She nodded, struck again by his understanding of her work process. "*Oui*, it can definitely be consuming. It can also be frustrating when things aren't coming together the way you want."

"I get that," he said, eyes flicking with understanding. "Sometimes I can see a design in my head, but it won't come out right on my computer and the harder I try, the bigger disaster it becomes. At times like that, I just have to step away, then come back at it with a different perspective."

Delphine nodded in agreement. "It sounds like we have some similar work experiences. Um, did you say you also design websites?"

"I do," he said, finishing off his ice cream cone.

"Would you be interested in taking a look at mine?" She was almost too embarrassed to ask, as her website was pathetically out of date. "My publisher's marketing team started a basic site, then turned it over to me. I have absolutely no idea what to do with it and it hasn't been updated in a long time."

"I sure can. Here." He pulled out a business card and handed it to her, along with a pen. "Why don't you write down your email address and website URL? I'll check it out, then email you to follow up."

"That would be wonderful." She scribbled the domain name and her business email address on the back of the card, then checked her watch before handing it back. A pang of disappointment hit her when she saw how much time had passed. "I have to get back to work."

"No problem. I should probably do the same," he replied, standing and turning to offer her assistance.

She took his proffered hand, allowing

him to pull her up. He held her hand for a moment longer as Hugo jumped around, tail wagging, excited to continue their walk.

"I enjoyed getting to know you better, Delphine," he said, squeezing her hand gently before releasing it.

Her heart sped up, hoping there would be a follow up invitation. "*Merci* for the coin experiment and ice cream," she said, trying not to get distracted by his eyes again.

"It was my pleasure. I'll email you soon. I hope your writing project goes well." He took a step back and broke the intimacy between them.

She bid him goodbye, gathered her hand bag and doggie treats, and left the flea market with Hugo leading the way toward home. Just before turning a corner, she glanced back for one last glimpse of Jean-Paul, but he was gone.

Gah, Delphine, get Jean-Paul out of your thoughts and jump back into your story. That's where your focus needs to be right now.

Focus, focus, focus.

But a set of brilliant blue eyes were never far from her thoughts.

CHAPTER FOUR

LATER THAT EVENING, Jean-Paul settled into the leather recliner in his living room. He responded to a text message from Angelique, who was traveling to visit the Simply Bella boutique in Paris.

Have a safe trip. Watch out for foreigners on the round-abouts! Let's catch up when you're back in La Rochelle.

Setting the cell phone aside, he turned the television to the current *La France Got Talent* episode for some background noise. If he had to spend the evening working, it was nice to at least have some entertainment to go with it. Once the application for his work email was open, he clicked through some messages from his father's office, answering questions about clients he had passed off to various representatives, all while listening to the judges' comments about the contestants.

With the emails completed, he pulled up

Delphine's website. She wasn't kidding about it being basic. It was hosted on a free platform, which was fine, but the website used an old template that wasn't responsive, which meant anyone viewing it on a tablet or cell phone would encounter a static page they would need to resize for readable fonts, as well as scroll from side to side to view all the elements. The only content was spotlights on her first two books, a bio page and a contact form. He pulled up Delphine's books on Amazon to compare to her website's book list. It looked like there were two more recent books missing from the site.

Opening a blank Word document, he began to work on a list, noting the books that needed to be updated. A general internet search for Delphine Baudry brought up social media pages and her blog, all of which he added to his notes document. He found several interviews and reviews that were highly ranked and added those links as well.

After reviewing the web pages and notes, he compiled a proposal for how his company could update her website, social media and online presence, and included sample links to work he'd done for other companies. He attached it to an email, then sent the message to Delphine with his cell phone number and a note that she could send him some dates and times to go over design elements if she wanted to move forward.

He also added a note that he'd enjoyed their experiment earlier that day and hoped to see her again soon.

With that task completed, he began reviewing notes for his upcoming meeting with Monsieur St. Germain. The savvy businessman had a long history with his father; the two once attended university together. Jean-Paul remembered business meetings and family gatherings from the time he was just a young boy. In fact, it was Monsieur St. Germain who encouraged his father to consider Jean-Paul's idea to open a new branch focused on website and social media marketing.

For that reason alone, Jean-Paul wanted to be sure this proposal was not just on par, but exceeded Monsieur St. Germain's expectations for Simply Bella's holiday season. It was worth the extra time to be prepared with ideas that showcased their winter sales or spotlighted select merchandise in a fresh way. He logged into their server to review back end code, making notes on what they could add or

41

tweak to create the new website elements. After logging out, he continued to put together a marketing plan for their social media presence with interactive giveaway ideas and discount incentives.

By the time he was done, he felt confident in the direction the proposal was going, *La France Got Talent* was long over, and his eyes needed a break from sorting through thousands of lines of code. As he closed programs, he found a return email from Delphine.

> *Jean-Paul,*
>
> *Ooh là là, there's a lot of work to be done! I like your proposal very much and would love to set up a meeting to review ideas. I need to make a trip to Bordeaux to meet with my editor, but am free next week on Monday or Wednesday afternoons. You can choose the time. If those days don't work, let me know.*
>
> *Thank you!*
>
> *Delphine*
>
> *PS - It's nice to find a fellow member of the geek department. =)*

Jean-Paul pulled up his calendar and saw he had a block of time free after his meeting with Simply Bella on Monday afternoon. He hit the email reply button.

Delphine,
Monday afternoon at three o'clock works for
me. *I hope your trip to Bordeaux is productive.*
See you next week, Miss Geek.
Jean-Paul

He closed the email interaction with Delphine, feeling a jumble of emotions. He couldn't seem to push back the growing sense of anticipation about meeting with her again.

If he was going to help with Delphine's website, he really should learn more about her writing. He went online and pulled up her Amazon Author page. Her first three books were sci-fi and speculative fiction twists on classic fairy tales. Her fourth book, The Space Corps General, looked like sci-fi with more of a romance element to it. He added the ebooks to his cart and checked out.

He started Delphine's first novel, a twist on the Alice in Wonderland story, after he had finished getting ready for bed. He plumped the pillows up and settled back against the bed frame as he clicked his way to the ebook's opening paragraph. He really wasn't a sci-fi guy. He never could get into all the made-up space stuff, but the descriptions in Delphine's novel were so vivid, it was like watching a movie in his head. The very determined Alice, the white rabbit in a space suit hopping through a black hole, and the robotic Cheshire cat just jumped off the page. It felt like if he opened the living room window, he would find them all lurking on the street outside his building.

As he continued reading, he imagined Delphine sitting at a table, her curls twisted up in knot as she brought Alice's story to life. He admired her talent to enchant others with her words. At that moment, his greatest desire was to discover what other traits made up this woman who came into his life in such a magical way.

CHAPTER FIVE

Friday, September 22nd

"DELPHINE, *MA BELLE*." Michel greeted her with a kiss to her cheek. "You are looking gorgeous, as usual."

Delphine's heart warmed. She had met many editors who simply complimented to schmooze their way into a client's good will and was grateful that her editor was sincere in not only his manuscript critiques, but also his compliments. Michel was all about fitness, which his physique clearly showed, even with his all-black attire. Combined with his dark eyes, hair and skin, she sometimes imagined him as a dark angel with a heart of gold, coming to rescue a legion of artists.

"I'm intrigued by this new book proposal," he said, leading her into his office. She took a seat on one end of the leather couch while he took the other end. On the coffee table, she could see a clipboard loaded up with print outs of her proposal, synopsis, and the first three chapters, covered with red markups and notes jotted in the margins. "How did you come up with the idea?"

"That's kind of a funny story, actually," she said, grabbing the bottle of water on the coffee table and twisting open the cap. "I wished for it." She took a generous sip of water.

Michel crossed his long legs, a bemused expression on his face. "Did you wish on a shooting star like Pinocchio?"

"Not quite. I made a wish on a coin and tossed it into a fountain. My coin ended up hitting another one and, I don't know, maybe it was the collision or something, but when I looked up at the guy who threw the other coin, the beginning scenes of the book popped into my head."

"And what happened with the guy?" Michel inquired.

"The guy?" Delphine squeaked out. "Why would you ask about him?"

Michel quirked an eyebrow. "Well, he was obviously important enough to mention when you told the story, so there must be some follow up. You know how dropping hints works in a novel. He sounds like a key element to your book."

"Um, no, I mean, he did toss the other coin, so that was important, right?" She leaned over and picked up her clipboard. "Shouldn't we talk about the book?"

Michel's lips twitched, as if trying not to laugh. Instead he picked up his clipboard set and pulled out his reading glasses. "Let's jump right in, shall we?"

Delphine pulled out her favorite purple editing pen, ready to mark away. Although she wasn't sure if she had dodged one bullet in exchange for another.

"I love the first three chapters. Obviously they're the first draft and changes will happen as we talk about more plot points, but they're solid. Great characterization, love the sensory elements you added to really make the New York City setting alive."

They continued through a review of those chapters, with their discussion centering more on the characters, their motivations, and other key points. Then they turned to the dreaded synopsis. Book titles weren't the only thing she stank at. Putting together a synopsis that didn't sound like, 'This happens, then that happens, oh and then this happens after that' was a horrific task.

"You're getting better with your synopsis

proposals," Michel said, peering at her over the rim of his reading glasses. "'Better' meaning you've made progress but still have a long way to go. Thankfully, we're able to get all the kinks out before I meet with the buying committee."

Delphine pulled up her mental armor around her tender writer's heart and prepared for critique mode, all while reminding herself that Michel's feedback was what helped strengthen her story. She took a deep breath, ready to dive in.

"First, let's talk about the overarching conflicts. We need to be sure that they don't snag any previous 'our world is dying' books out there."

And so it began. Over the next hour, they thoroughly went through conflicts, resolutions, setting, and details behind the science of it all. For as much as Michel nit-picked and pulled apart the synopsis, Delphine pushed back with details that were in her notes or stuck in her head. The back and forth led to a plot with more depth and strength.

It was exhausting but oh-so-rewarding by the time the meeting ended.

"Are you staying in Bordeaux tonight or heading back to La Rochelle?" Michel asked as they gathered their notes together.

"Staying. I have to recover from our meeting so I don't have heart failure on the train," Delphine responded.

Michel's hearty laugh filled the room. "Excellent. Have dinner with Bernice and me this evening. There's a new restaurant we've been wanting to check out, and Bernice would love to get out of cooking . . . And I'm sure she'll get you to spill more details about that wishing fountain story."

Delphine's laugh fell flat, knowing Michel's comment about his wife's prying skills was true. "I would love to spend the evening with you both. What time and where shall we meet?"

"How about I send a company car to pick you up about seven o'clock?" Michel suggested.

With the details agreed upon, Delphine returned to her hotel on foot. She needed the walk and fresh air to allow the full impact of the meeting to sink in. While her book plot was stronger, there were still elements that bothered her. She just wished she could figure out how to fix them. She pulled out her cell phone and tapped on the button for her parent's home. It rang a few times before going to voicemail.

"*Bonjour*, Maman. I just finished a meeting with Michel and wanted to tell you

49

all about it. He loved Candessa and Felix, but I'm still struggling with—" She stumbled to a stop, her throat clogging up, remembering that Maman wasn't going to hear the message because the voices and names confused her too much, so only Papa checked voicemail now. She swallowed past the thick lump, then pushed out her next few words. "I'm sorry, Papa. Force of habit, I suppose. I hope you and Maman are well. Call me when you can. Love you."

She ended the call, using all her will to force back the scald of tears.

She held it together just long enough to make it to the elevator before the first sob escaped. She bit her lip hard, trying to think of anything else until she reached the safety of her hotel room, where all the emotions took over.

She hated this horrible disease and how it ripped her Maman out of her life.

CHAPTER SIX

Monday, September 25th

JEAN-PAUL RUBBED HIS FOREHEAD, trying to keep his patience with Angelique St. Germain as she continued to go over her vision for Simply Bella in excruciating detail, firmly putting their meeting ten minutes over schedule. He was rather annoyed that Mr. St. Germain had delegated the meeting to his daughter without informing him. As much as he adored his long-time friend, he was frustrated that the attempts to pair them together had now moved from social events into his business affairs. It was immensely difficult to keep his cool.

When she finally finished her spiel, he simply smiled because he certainly didn't want to say anything to add to the length of their meeting.

"*Très bien*. That sums up the meeting," he said. He stood and moved to the other side of the desk from where she sat in her fashionable suit with an inappropriately short skirt, avoiding the hurt look in her eyes. There was a slight kick in the gut for being less than a friend should be, but he'd just have to make it up to her later. "I'll have my secretary call when the next version is ready to be approved before going live."

Her eyebrows scrunched together as she processed the quick ending of their meeting. "But there's still more for us to discuss."

"I'm sorry, Angelique. I thought I was meeting with your father, so I scheduled our normal time block. I didn't realize we'd need an extended appointment. We can reschedule to continue the conversation, but my next appointment is waiting."

He opened the office door, hoping to usher her out. Instead she sauntered across the room, stopping just short of the door. When he extended his hand, she took it, then leaned up on her toes to leave lingering *bise* kisses on each of his cheeks before slightly stepping back. The strong scent of her jasmine perfume wafted around him like a dense cloud, causing his eyes to water as he resisted the urge to sneeze.

"*Merci beaucoup*, Jean-Paul. I look forward to seeing the designs soon." Her ruby red lips spread into a coy smile before she pivoted and sashayed out of the office.

"Monsieur Chassériau. Your next appointment is here," his secretary said, motioning to the couch in the waiting area.

Jean-Paul turned to greet Delphine. "I'm sorry about the wait."

"It's fine, I was able to jot down some notes while I waited." As she passed Helena's desk, she pulled out a few tissues and handed them to him, then gestured to her cheek.

He groaned, ushering her into his office before closing the door. He invited her to sit down, but stopped at a small mirror on the shelves before he joined her. And there it was, red lipstick smeared on not one, but both of his cheeks. It took some work, but he finally got both messes cleaned up. Or at least he hoped he did. The burning sensation that reddened his cheeks from the embarrassing display wasn't helping.

"I'm sorry about that," he said, returning to his desk.

"No problem. Is she a new client?" Delphine inquired, looking relaxed and all too composed compared to the jumbled mess he was at the moment.

"No, our families are close, and we grew up seeing each other a few times each year. Our fathers have worked together for as long as I can remember. I usually meet with her father, but it seems she might be the new company liaison."

"Hmm," Delphine murmured, twisting her hands together before tucking them at her sides, as if trying to hold something in.

He folded his arms and leaned forward onto his desk. "You should just say whatever is on your mind."

She shook her head. "That never goes very well."

Her comment made him laugh, and he relaxed for the first time since Angelique left. He sank back into his chair, his full attention on her. "No, truly, go ahead."

She twisted her hands together again. "Well," she started. "It's just that as an author, I spend a lot of time studying people, their personalities, reactions to others and situations. But what I observe can be wrong too because it's taken out of context rather than seeing the full picture."

"I've known Angelique my entire life, but we have only recently spent more than a week or two together. When we were children, I spent more time with her brothers."

"Have you ever asked her out for a date?" She gasped, then flushed a delicate pink. "I'm sorry, I know that's a personal question. You don't have to answer it," she said, waving her hand as if it could erase that part of their conversation.

He couldn't help but feel pleased by her reaction to asking personal questions. He suppressed a smile and shrugged nonchalantly. "I don't mind. And no, I haven't. Her family has invited me to several social functions since I moved to La Rochelle, but it's purely platonic."

Delphine tilted her head in consideration. "Are you sure she doesn't consider them dates? She's obviously interested in you. Considering what you said and assuming you have been a bit stand-offish, like you were at the door just now, I'd say she's set you in her sights."

He rubbed his hand across his face, taking in the confirmation of his speculation about Angelique's hopes for their relationship.

"Does that surprise you?" Delphine asked.

"No, it worries me. I had a feeling she might be angling for us to pair up, but I was hoping if I kept things strictly friendly, the efforts would cool off. So what you're saying is, my strategy is having the opposite effect?"

Delphine shrugged. "That would be my guess, from what I just observed. And that bothers you. Interesting."

He wasn't sure he liked how she said that last word. "Why do you say that?"

She shrugged again. He didn't think he liked it when she did that either. "It's just generally assumed that men prefer women like Angelique. She's all that Vanity Fair says beauty is—gorgeous platinum blonde hair with a sun-kissed tan. She's into fashion, keeps up with the trends, and has a to-die-for body."

He mulled over what she said. "That's all true, if you buy into what the media portrays to be beautiful and desirable. There are certainly both men and women who get caught up in what others think in that realm, but I believe there's a greater number of people who look for just the opposite."

"They look for someone ugly?" she asked, her lips turning up at one corner.

"No." He paused, trying to figure out how to say the words without sounding too cheesy. "My Papa taught us to look for a heart that blends with ours. It didn't matter if belongs to a friend, a co-worker, or a love interest. When you search their hearts, you find a friend for life. While I know others may not use that phrasing to define their search, I do think it's basically what they are searching for."

"Kindred spirits," Delphine said, as if letting the words soak in.

"Yes, that's one way you could say it."

"Anne of Green Gables," she mumbled, then started digging through her bag. She pulled out a familiar notebook and pen and started writing.

"Are you in brainstorming mode again?" he asked, amused by her reaction.

She shushed him and continued to write a few more sentences, then quickly scanned them before closing her notebook. When her attention returned to him, he was struck by how bright and alive her light brown eyes were.

"Sometimes something strikes me and I have to jot it down before it disappears," she apologized. "So no Angelique?"

"*Non*, not for me."

Her smile warmed, and their eyes held for a moment without any additional words passing between them. She flushed a charming pink color again and ducked her head, her curls tumbling forward to partially cover her face.

"Perhaps we can chat about your website now?" he suggested.

Delphine pulled her chair closer to his desk, and he turned the monitor to face her. He opened a digital folder to show her samples of logos and website layouts he mocked up. She oohed and hmmed as she viewed the samples, but in the end, she was very decisive about the designs she liked best. She filled out information so he could incorporate all her social media, newsletter, and other links on the website.

His secretary buzzed the line to let him know his next appointment had arrived. Their meeting was over all too soon. Before he opened the door for Delphine to leave, he paused. "The Musée d'Art is having a special Classic Hollywood display this week. I was thinking about going to see it Wednesday evening. Would you be interested in joining me?"

"It sounds like fun, but I have a deadline I need to hit by Wednesday evening," she said.

"Of course, that's fine. No problem," he said, trying to cover up his disappointment and the awkwardness of being turned down. He reached out to turn the doorknob when Delphine placed her hand over his. He stilled, turning to meet her sincere eyes.

"But I could go Thursday," she prompted.

A whoosh of air escaped his lungs. He hadn't realized he was holding his breath. "Thursday is *fantastique*. Seven o'clock? We could go to the exhibit, then get dessert afterward."

"Perfect. I'll see you then," she said, a beautiful smile brightening her eyes.

He signaled for a short break to his secretary after Delphine left. He closed his office door and leaned back against it. He did it. He asked one of the most intriguing women he'd ever met out on an official date. He placed his hand over his heart. It thrummed with excitement because, so far, it recognized a friend for life . . . and possibly something even more precious.

CHAPTER SEVEN

Thursday, September 28th

DELPHINE RUBBED HER DAMP PALMS on the sides of her jeans, then tried to open the tube of mascara again. Darn the lotion she just put on! She loved the cherry-vanilla scent, but it was seriously bad timing when it came to putting on makeup. She twisted as hard as she could. The cap not only gave way, but it came all the way out of the tube, smearing mascara across her hand. Gah! She quickly set the tube and wand aside to wash her hands before the black mess stained her skin.

Okay, Delphine, you can do this, she thought while drying her hands. It's just a date. With Jean-Paul. Who was also not only scrumptious to look at, but nothing like the slew of one-dimensional men she'd previously dated who had nothing to talk about besides the latest contenders for the World Cup and upcoming wine tours.

She picked the mascara back up and applied a smooth coating to each set of eyelashes. She finished her primping by swiping on some berry colored lip gloss. Then she gathered her hair into a loose ponytail and pulled out a few tendrils to curl around her face. Braiding the ponytail and twisting it around the base, she created a cute messy bun to complete the look. She stepped back to check her appearance.

Cute dark jeans. Check. Black fitted shirt layered with her favorite lacy charcoal gray cardigan. Check. Makeup and hair. Check, check.

She added some money, apartment keys, phone, and lip gloss into a wristlet and checked her hair one last time to make sure she was all ready. She glanced toward the clock, but a knock sounded at the door.

He's here! She pressed her hand to her abdomen to quiet the anticipation fluttering around while Hugo raced to the door, bark, bark, barking to defend them from intruders. She sent a silent plea to the heavens that this evening would go well.

She scooped up the wriggly Hugo, then opened the door. She was captivated once again by Jean-Paul's blue eyes and the sparkle of anticipation that she saw reflected there.

"*Bonjour*, Jean-Paul," she greeted him. "Please come in."

"You look *très belle*," he said, stepping into her apartment. He brought his arm from behind his back and presented a beautiful bouquet of white daisies, yellow roses, and sunflowers. "I saw these, and they reminded me of how happy you look when you're writing."

"That's the most wonderful compliment. *Merci*," she replied, putting Hugo down to accept the gift. She leaned up on her toes and placed a *bise* kiss on his cheek. The light fresh scent of his cologne, mixed with the warmth of his skin, sent a flush through her. She pulled back and tripped over Hugo as he paced between them. Jean-Paul quickly grabbed her elbow to steady her, bringing them quite close together. Kissably close, she thought as a warm rush of tingles spread through her. "Um, I'll put these in a vase. It will just take a minute."

She left him to wander around her tiny living room while she quickly pulled a vase out of the cupboard, filled it with water, and added the flowers. She took a deep breath, hoping to cool the flurry of emotions tangling about inside before she brought the arrangement back out into the living room and placed it on her desk.

"I assume this is where all the magic happens," Jean-Paul said, indicating the desk.

"Well, I mostly do my monthly bills here," she admitted. "I like to move around when I work, so I have several writing nooks in the apartment."

He turned in a circle, taking in the areas of her living space that he could see. "Do you have a spot you prefer?"

"Mmm–*oui*," she murmured, motioning toward the other side of the room. "One of my favorites is the overstuffed chair and ottoman over by the window. I enjoy the natural sunlight in the afternoon."

"Jobs like ours can sometimes mean being chained to a stuffy office. I try to plan a few afternoons each week to do design work away from the office, usually somewhere outside. A spot like this is a nice option, too. I've been reading your books, by the way."

"You have?" she asked, surprised by his admission. Should she ask the question every author dreaded? She bit her lip, then plunged ahead. "What did you think?"

Her hands twisted and clenched together as she waited for his answer. It was never fun to hear a friend say he enjoyed your book, but have you read so-and-so's because it was amazing. Or that they couldn't get into it. Or to have a friend go total fan crazy about your characters to the point that it took over every single conversation. There didn't seem to ever be a happy middle ground. Especially when all she wanted to hear was that he liked her writing.

Jean-Paul picked up the funky rock paperweight on her desk and fiddled with it. "First, I have to admit that I've tried other sci-fi books my friends have recommended, but could never get into them."

Oh no, here it came. Their first official date may end before it even got a chance to begin.

"But I started with your twist on the Alice in Wonderland fairy tale. The way you weaved the story to make the sci-fi elements as real as everyday life pulled me in. I finished the book impressed with your talent to create scenes that portray the magic in your imagination."

Handsome guy + understanding of the creative brain = girl's mind totally blown.

Definitely a good kick-off to their evening.

That was the beginning of a conversation that flowed smoothly as they walked toward the *Musée d'Art*. The evening rays from the sun cast a beautiful orangey-yellow glow against the old buildings. The breeze held an underlying coolness that was just on the edge of comfortable versus chilly. As they walked, their arms occasionally bumped into each other, bring their hands within holding distance. Delphine's breath caught, wondering if he might take the initiative and take her hand in his. Unfortunately, they arrived at the *Musée* too soon to find out.

She was surprised by the number of attendees who filled the halls. She had no idea it would be such a popular exhibit. She turned her attention back to Jean-Paul, who was adorable as he studied the exhibit map.

"I think if we start here," he said, pointing to a spot on the map, "we can view the formal Hollywood star portraits, then cut through this exhibit here and end with the movie posters. What do you think?"

She nodded her agreement. Happy tingles cascaded through her when he placed his hand on her lower back. His guidance as they weaved through the crowd made her feel protected and safe, nestled near his side as they moved from picture to picture. As they perused the formal portrait gallery, she could tell from the way Jean-Paul tilted his head from side-to-side that he saw something more than simply photos of movie stars hanging on the wall.

"What is it you're looking for, Jean-Paul?"

His eyebrows crunched together. "I'm not sure I can explain it very well, but I'll try. You've used a digital camera before, right?"

She lifted her phone up and lightly laughed, embarrassed to admit the simplicity of her photography skills. "If you count this one, then yes."

"*Oui*," Jean-Paul said, nodding. "That is what most of our society considers photography now. Point, shoot, upload it to your favorite photo editor, add some filters, then share it with your friends via social media."

"That pretty much sums up my abilities," she said, flirtatiously linking her arm with his as they navigated around a small group. She bit her lip, wondering if she was too bold, but her fears melted away when he put his hand over hers where it rested in the crook of his arm. Walking together, being beside one another, felt so natural, comfortable, like they had been doing it forever. She may enjoy the drama and adventure of writing for teenagers, but at this moment, she definitely preferred the magic and butterflies that came with an intriguing romance.

"These portraits were taken before the digital era. When photographers spent months or even years learning how to combine the mechanical functions of their camera with various filters and balancing light and shadows to create something unique, a signature style. Some photographers used more creativity in the dark room to over or under expose their photographs to achieve the final touches. It was an era when photography truly was an art form." He pointed to two different portraits and explained in terms she could understand what the differences were. Once she grasped the photographic concepts, she was able to pick out unique elements here and there to discuss.

He stopped abruptly near the entrance to the next exhibit. The set up of the room made a bottleneck with a long line of people backed up and overflowing into the halls.

"Perhaps we'll skip this one," Jean-Paul suggested. "If it clears out, we can always return later."

She agreed, and they navigated around the crush in the middle exhibit and went directly to the movie posters, where they contrasted the design elements between portrait photography to classic movie posters, then again the classic movie posters to modern poster designs.

"This has been fascinating, Jean-Paul. I've discovered a whole new appreciation for photography," she admitted.

"I'm glad you came. It was nice to share it with someone willing to put up with my artistic side," he said, leading them back out into the lobby area where it was much less crowded.

"Would you like to—," she started, but was cut off when someone called her name from across the lobby. They both turned and found a group of two men and a woman coming toward them.

"Pablo, Henrik, and Viv," Delphine said, laughing with delight. "How are you?"

"We thought that was you," Pablo responded, wrapping her up in a big hug and placing loud smacking kisses on her cheeks before he nudged her on to their other friends for more of the same.

"It's been forever since we've seen you, sweetheart. Who's your chap, eh?" Henrik inquired, lifting his brows up and down multiple times.

Delphine stepped back and took her date's arm. "Jean-Paul, I'd like to introduce you to a group of the craziest writers I know. Pablo Bonadio, Henrik Safford, and Viv

Zapata," she said, going right down the row. Jean-Paul greeted each with a hand shake.

"So what do you write?" he asked.

"Steampunk and dragons for kids," Pablo replied.

"Biographies and historical nonfiction for me," Henrik said with a nod.

Viv just smiled, all sassy with a hand propped on her hip. "I specialize in romances," Viv said while Pablo and Henrik chuckled. Delphine knew the act well, especially since most people who met female writers assumed they wrote romance. "Except one of my lovers tends to end up dead while the other is on the run from a certain homicide detective."

"Gruesome novels, they are. Don't know why so many people snatch the nasty things up," Henrik lamented, shaking his head. "People need to fill their brains with more substance."

"You just say that because you wish you had thought up Rebecca Jones first," Viv responded.

"Don't we all?" Pablo replied.

"But what would we do with Rebecca?" Delphine responded. "I'd send her into space, Pablo would have her riding mechanical dragons, and Henrik would write her memoir. No, I think Rebecca can

69

only be Rebecca as Viv's creation."

"Too true, Del. Too true," Henrik responded with a wry smile.

"And this is why we miss you. When are you coming to Spain to visit?" Pablo asked.

"Spain? I thought you were in Paris," Delphine said.

"Henrik and I moved to Spain when he was offered a contract for an absurdly rich man's biography. The interviews will take place in Madrid. We just popped up to visit Viv for the week on holiday," Pablo said.

"Well, I'm glad you did. It has been too long since we last saw each other. What was it, two years ago at the Expo in Germany?"

Viv draped her arm across Henrik's shoulder. "What I remember is dragging you with us to the discothèque."

Delphine giggled nervously. "What I remember is you and Henrik busting some serious moves on the dance floor, while Pablo and I stayed safely tucked away in a booth and had our own little brainstorming session."

Henrik clapped his hands together, bouncing up and down. "Ooh! Let's do it again!"

Delphine shook her head from side to side. "I have a book deadline coming up."

"Pish posh. That excuse doesn't work on

us, dear." Viv batted her long lashes and focused her attention on Jean-Paul. "Do you enjoy dancing?"

"I've been to my fair share of discothèques. In fact, the White Rabbit here in La Rochelle has an incredible DJ with a good mix of hip hop and electro dance mixes. Plus Friday and Saturday nights, ladies get in free."

"Would you seriously go?" Delphine asked Jean-Paul skeptically.

"If you were my date, absolutely," he replied without hesitation.

Henrik nudged Pablo with his elbow. "She's a goner," he pseudo-whispered, and Pablo nodded in agreement.

"Just give in, Del. There's no way you'll get out of it now," Viv teased.

"Okay, fine," Delphine said, throwing up her hands in defeat. "But I really do have a deadline, so I can't go until Friday."

"Excellent. I'll call to reserve a table," Viv said. "Shall we meet for dinner at nine-thirty?"

"I'll take care of the dinner reservations and text you all the details," Delphine said, feeling the need to take charge of something.

"Marvelous," Henrik replied. "We'll see you next week."

CHAPTER EIGHT

JEAN-PAUL SMILED as Delphine was caught up in a flurry of *bise* kisses from her friends before they were once again alone.

She turned to him and pressed her hands to her flushed cheeks. "Did that really just happen?"

She looked so cute and flustered by the turn of events. "It definitely did." He took her hand and twirled her in an impromptu circle. "And I can't wait to get you out on the dance floor."

A squeak escaped her lips as she stumbled over her feet. He pulled her into an embrace to help her catch her balance. There they were, in a repeat position of earlier in the evening, only this time felt more intimate. Heat rushed through him as he held her, her wide eyes glimmering up at him, revealing that she was just as affected by their nearness as he was.

"D-d-don't blame me when I crush your toes," she said, a slight smile curving her lips upward.

"If there are more happy accidents like this one, then it will be worth it." He winked before stepping back. "Shall we go?"

When she nodded, he threaded her hand through the crook of his elbow, amazed again how just that simple touch made him happy. They left the lights of the *Musée* for the dimness of the evening and came to an abrupt halt on the marble steps when they were met by yet another acquaintance.

"Oh, Jean-Paul, *mon chéri*. How wonderful to run into you," Angelique said as she and her crew of wealthy friends ascended the steps. They all wore various versions of skimpy black dresses, although Angelique's was the most risqué of them all, with a plunging neckline that went almost to her navel. Her long blonde hair was artfully arranged to cascade over one shoulder, drawing attention from her neck down to her cleavage.

She plastered herself up against him to kiss his cheek, leaving behind a strong mixture of her jasmine perfume and wine. He grasped her elbows to steady the giggly Angelique before taking a step to the side, making sure to keep Delphine beside him. "Delphine, this is my friend, Angelique. She is also the daughter of my client, Monsieur St. Germain of the Simply Bella clothing boutiques."

"Of course," Delphine said. "I recognize you from Simply Bella's spring/summer show at fashion week in Paris. I love the new vintage-twist collection."

Angelique's gaze roamed from head to toe, giving Delphine a quick once-over before giggling some more and extending a wobbly hand. "So nice to meet a friend of Jean-Paul's. My family and I have monopolized so much of his time, it's nice to know he's expanding into some other . . . social circles."

Delphine stiffened beside him as she quickly shook Angelique's hand. He felt the need to move on sooner rather than later. "We just finished with the exhibit. I'm sure you and your friends will find it quite fascinating. We don't want to keep you out in the chilly air," he said, intending to say good evening.

"Yes, come on already," one of her friends whined, pulling at Angelique's arm and upsetting her balance.

"Whoopsie." Angelique grabbed onto him as she found her footing again. Her face tipped up toward his, her smile slightly tipsy too. "It's too bad you're not alone so you could join us for a more entertaining tour. But no matter, I'll see you Sunday for the family dinner." She finally released his arm and gave a little wave. *"Au revoir*, Daphne," she said.

He nodded farewell to her friends, then ushered Delphine away. The silence between them was thick until they were well out of ear shot.

"I'm sorry, Angelique normally isn't like that," he began, but Delphine cut him off.

"Did you see the way she looked at me? Like I was chopped meat to be thrown to the dogs. Well, let me tell you what, little miss not-so-charming, I'm prime rib. No, I'm even better than prime rib, whatever cut of meat that is. Spoiled little brat," she murmured under her breath before pivoting to face him. "And did I say anything? No. I just stood there with a million let-me-kick-your-butt-to-the-curb comments running through my head, because she's not my client. Oh no, thank the heavens for that." Delphine sucked in a deep breath, almost growling as she said, "Expanding your social circles, my butt."

He tried to hold it in, but a sputtering laugh escaped. He even tried to cover it up by faking a cough, but once one laugh escaped, another quickly followed. It didn't help that Delphine put her hand on her hip and one foot was tapping, up and down, like a disapproving school teacher.

"Are you laughing at me?" she asked. "Because I can go back and send Angelique over so you can enjoy the remainder of the evening together."

"Don't be cruel. Truly, I think she was a bit sloshed," he said. He put his hand on her shoulder, doing his best to suck back the laughter, but his shoulders betrayed him by shaking with mirth. "Did you really attend fashion week?"

"No, a few of my friends attend each year and I heard about Simply Bella's new line from them. Plus, hello, YouTube recaps everything." She reached up, rubbing her thumb over his cheek. "She did it again. She's determined to mark you for her own."

Jean-Paul dug in his pocket and pulled out a tissue, then handed it to her. She swiped at his cheek a few more times. He breathed in the tangy fruit scent of her lotion and briefly closed his eyes. He wished for the scent to sink into his memory, knowing that whenever he encountered it in the future, he'd be reminded of this evening and all of the connections and feelings that were building between them.

"I think I got the worst of it," she said,

her voice softer. Her eyes met his, looking contrite and serious. "I'm sorry about what I said. When I get mad, I tend to rant without thinking first."

He captured her hand, playing with her delicate fingers. "I understand. Besides, I agree. You're definitely prime rib worthy."

Her face flushed a deep pink. "I can't believe I said that. I need a verbal editor before I speak."

He chuckled. "I rather like the unedited version of you." He kept her hand in his as they continued walking again. "Are you still up for dessert?"

She gently squeezed his hand. "A café sounds wonderful."

The tables were mostly full at Chez Marguerite, but they were able to snag a spot in a secluded corner. Their conversation was as rich as the crème brûlée they shared, the topics running through their shared enjoyment of various sciences. One moment they discussed satellites and discoveries in the universe, then the next talked about polar bears and their habitat. Delphine shared an experience she had while on tour the previous summer in Norway.

"Having the opportunity to be in Norway for work, there was no way I was going to pass up a side trip to Svalbard. The hiking expedition to see the polar bears was mind-bending. They are so beautiful and majestic on television and in print, but neither of those can compare to observing them in their natural habitats. That trip is definitely up in my top five explorations."

"What was your favorite trip?" he asked.

"Ugh, that's such a hard one." She paused, tapping her finger on her chin. "Okay, I'll give you my top five, but I'm not ranking them."

He leaned forward, ready to hear more about her adventures.

"The polar bears in Norway, so that's one," she said, ticking it off on her fingers. "Did you know there's a petrified forest in Arizona?"

Delphine pulled out her phone. As she tapped her way to find an album, the blonde curls that framed her face fell forward. The dim lighting in the room glinted off her hair, making them look like buttery vanilla. He wished he could reach out and touch them to see if they were as soft as they looked. Thankfully, she turned the phone around and pulled his thoughts back to the moment. The photos of the Petrified Forest prompted a discussion of its unique ecological system.

"Have you been to Pompeii?" he asked.

She shivered. "No, just the thought of seeing all those people frozen in ash like that, it's a little more than I can handle. I may love science, but I have a light stomach when it comes to terrible things like that."

Mental notation #27: Don't invite Delphine to scary movie marathons. As much as he'd enjoy her burying her head in his shoulder during the freaky parts, being the reason she might end up with nightmares wasn't a good dating strategy.

"Let's see, number three would be attending a space shuttle launch at Kennedy Space Center in Florida. My father splurged and took our family on that trip. Touring the space center museums, then watching the launch from the viewing island closest to the launch pad was awe-inspiring."

"Astronomy was one of my favorite subjects in school, but I've always wanted to see a space shuttle," he admitted.

"The experience is a million times better in person. I've had friends attend satellite launches since then and they say even those smaller launches are amazing. Have you ever thought about planning a trip to Florida to see the Atlantis space shuttle? They have it on display there now."

"It's on my bucket list," he said, then turned the conversation back to her list. "So

I'm waiting for number four and five."

"Well, they are both right here in our home country."

"Let me guess," he said. "Paris is one of them."

"Paris is a wonderful city with lots of history, but for me, it's too busy. No, number four is the Loire Valley. I love the river, the castles, the arched bridges, the gardens, the villages . . . Honestly, I could go on and on. I feel like Cinderella whenever I go there," she said, a dreamy tone to her voice.

"Stuck in an attic and forced to be a maid?" he joked.

"No, silly," she said, swatting at his hand. "It inspires a feeling of happily ever after. Have you been there?"

He shook his head. "I haven't, but your description of it certainly intrigues me."

Her cheeks flushed with a pretty pink tinge. "We should plan a trip the Loire Valley sometime. I would love to show you my favorite spots."

"That's a trip I would very much enjoy." He smiled, definitely liking how their conversation turned to talking about future plans to share together.

Delphine propped her elbow on the table, tucking her chin into the palm of her

80

hand. "That brings us to number five, which is right here. La Rochelle."

"Really? But you already live here. Does that count?"

"Who says you can't live in the one place you would choose over anywhere else?" She covered a yawn, then straightened in her seat.

It was past midnight. Time to get the princess home before she wilted. "How about you tell me more about it as I walk you home?"

The night air was brisk and Delphine shivered when they stepped out of the café. He loved the way she threaded her arm through his and leaned close as they walked, their bodies brushing against each other and sparking plenty of warmth between them. Delphine continued their conversation, talking about her time in Switzerland and how she dreamed of returning to La Rochelle and how the towers were her symbol of home. They talked more about places they'd like to visit both in France and abroad until they arrived at her front door.

"Thank you for coming to the exhibit," he said, giving in and reaching up to twirl one of the curls with a finger. They felt like silk threads as the locks slid over his skin. Her head tilted toward him as his fingers skimmed over her cheek, relishing the softness. He wished he could continue the trail past her ear and down her neck, maybe sink his fingers into her hair where it was twisted in the back. Instead he retreated, keeping himself in check. It was, after all, still their first date.

"I had a wonderful evening," Delphine said, her cheeks flushed a gentle pink.

"Me, too. I hope your writing goes well over the next few days. I'm looking forward to our date to the discothèque."

Delphine groaned. "I'll definitely be holed up the next few days, but you're welcome to text me. I tend to leave my phone on silent and randomly check it during the day when I take stretching breaks."

He wriggled his eyebrows. "In that case, may our phones become the best of friends."

She laughed, which Hugo must've heard, because he began barking on the other side of the door.

"I better go before he wakes the neighbors," she said.

"Of course. *Bon nuit*," he said, placing his hand at her waist, then leaning in.

She gripped his arm, her eyes never leaving his face.

Oh, how he wanted to place his lips on hers, to linger there for just a breath. Instead he placed a soft kiss to her cheek, her curls brushing against his face. Her lips brushed his cheek, returning the kiss. Just that simple exchange had his heart jumping, thumping against his chest. He pulled back, taking her hand from his arm and placing a kiss on her inner-wrist, feeling her pulse thrumming fast like his.

Her beautiful brown eyes were round and soft as she whispered goodnight and slipped inside.

All of the warmth from the moment before swooshed and left the hallway empty and lonely. Jean-Paul rubbed his hand on his chest, just over his heart. Had she captured that piece of him already?

CHAPTER NINE

Friday, September 29th

DELPHINE PUSHED AWAY from her desk. She needed to a break from Candessa and Felix. The two just were not cooperating with her plan for their story, the little brats. There was something she missed, something essential to their story that needed to be changed. If only she could figure out what that something was sooner rather than later. Most certainly it needed to be before she threw her laptop across the room.

"Hugo," she called, waking him up from his spot on the couch where he was napping. "Who wants to play?"

His little tail wagged like crazy as he jumped down and darted to his stuffed animal of the week. As they played tug of war, she noted the poor stuffed giraffe had already lost an ear and a leg. She was pretty sure today was going to be the day Hugo ripped the body apart and gutted out all the stuffing, making the living room look like a mini-snowstorm invaded it. When Hugo allowed her to win the tug of war, he hunched down and growled until she threw it across the room for him to fetch, then he proudly returned to start the game all over again. After they were both sufficiently played out, Delphine grabbed her phone to check her messages.

She smiled when she saw a photo message from Jean-Paul. He had been exploring bits of La Rochelle each day and sending her pics of his discoveries. Today he was in the area near the port. She clicked on his text, then laughed when she saw his message and accompanying pictures of the Lectores statue.

Freakiest wall of writers I've ever seen. I hope they don't cast you in bronze like this.

She tapped on the reply box, her thumbs doing their magic on the tiny keyboard before sending back a reply.

It's actually a wall of readers, so beware. They may be looking for their next victim to immortalize.

She scrolled to her next message, which

was from her editor Michel.

The buying committee loved your book pitch. They want to know dates so they can set a production schedule.

Delphine rubbed her chest, anxiety rushing through her. Dates, hard-core deadlines that were more than just pushing through the rough draft. She consulted the wall calendar in the kitchen, flipping through the months, trying to figure out realistic time frames.

She needed to get through this first draft, then another round of rewrites before she sent it on to her alpha readers, so that put her at the end of October. Then another round of rewrites before the manuscript would go to her beta readers at the end of November. With it being the holidays, she wouldn't get the manuscript back until January. Those rewrites shouldn't be as time intensive, so she could get that manuscript to the professional editor she hired to rip her manuscript to shreds around mid-January. That round of editing was always killer, so she probably wouldn't be done with it until March. And then she'd have one final set of fresh eyes to make sure she hadn't messed up anyone's names and that the story still flowed smoothly.

She felt confident about a mid-to-end of April time frame for Michel to receive the manuscript. From that point, he would schedule all the publisher in-house editing rounds and actual publication details.

She rubbed her chest again, letting out a heavy sigh. The actual planning of all the work that went into a novel exhausted her. Sometimes she missed the days when she simply wrote to fulfill her own creative desires.

She clicked on Michel's text and replied with her own tentative date for when the manuscript should arrive in his email box.

Another message from Jean-Paul popped up. *How's Candessa treating you today?*

His question brought a smile to her face. She discovered that she could chat with him about her characters and Jean-Paul didn't think it odd that the imaginary people in her head were real to her, battling for her time to create their stories.

She's being a feisty chick. Not getting along with Felix at all. My hands are getting tired from all the deleting and rewriting.

She clicked send, and a message from Michel came through.

If there's any way to bump that turn-in date to the beginning of March, that would be ideal.

Grrr. Ideal for him sure, she thought, her hand coming up to rub away the anxiety again. She loved her editor and knew he'd work with her on the time frame, but still . . . stress!

Her phone vibrated and a message from Jean-Paul popped up.

My hands would be happy to come over and give a massage to your hands.

That sounded divine. Her phone vibrated again just as she tapped out a quick response and hit send.

*Perhaps our hands should schedule a date. Mine quite miss yours. *winky face**

Her phone vibrated again. This time it was a picture from Jean-Paul of the Tour de la Lanterne. She always thought it was the weirdest tower at the port with its funky pointed dome. It always reminded her of those ugly paper party hats.

Check out this tower. It's almost looks like a rocket ship, don't you think?

A message came through from Michel again. He must really want to talk more about the book deadline, she thought. She tapped on the message.

I had no idea our hands had become so intimately acquainted. Should I let Bernice in on our secret?

What the? She scrolled up. No. Oh no, no, no.

She had sent the text for Jean-Paul to her editor!

Um, sheesh, what did she say now?

Sorry about that, she typed. *Wrong recipient.*

Seriously, what else could she say? She was mortified. While Michel had tried to pry into her personal life on her last visit—and yes, Bernice was a masterful accomplice on that count—she generally kept things fairly professional between them.

And what did Jean-Paul think about her not responding? She quickly copied and pasted the original message and sent it to the correct person, then silenced her phone and set it aside. She'd look at it again on her next break. She needed some distance from all the embarrassment.

"All right, Candessa, let's get this worked out."

Delphine sat down at the computer and opened a blank document. She needed to do some free range brainstorming to figure out where the story was going wrong.

She began typing, starting with the characters. But she felt like they were well developed and not the problem, so she moved onto the conflicts, putting her thoughts on the screen. Most of the conflicts were spot on, but a few were falling flat. Why? What wasn't working? As she continued writing her thoughts out, she came to the setting. She had set their location in futuristic New York City, where technology was the king and only the elite of the elite lived. As she worked her way through it, the picture of the Tour de la Lanterne popped into her head.

She paused, sucking her bottom lip between her teeth and nibbling at it. The tower did have some rocket-like similarities to it, even with its ancient history.

What if . . .

What if a scientist long ago was centuries ahead of his time? What if he built a secret lower level of the tower with rocket capabilities to be developed in the future? And what if it was abandoned and forgotten about until a dystopian society discovered the plans, developed the capabilities, and was now forced to use the rocket as a means for the elite to escape a planet they thought was dying?

Her mind spun and whirled with the possibilities as she brainstormed and developed the new setting. It was refreshing to develop the story in a city she loved rather than one she thought would appeal to her readers. Suddenly, the story had new life. It was coming together in a way she least expected. Thank goodness for Jean-Paul and his fresh perspective. She couldn't wait to tell him about this new twist in her story development.

CHAPTER TEN

Monday, October 2nd

JEAN-PAUL MADE SOME final adjustments to Delphine's website, then clicked to test all the links, pages, and interactive elements until he was satisfied it all came together in a way that drew in her fans.

He pulled out his phone and went to the server link to also test out the compatibility for phone screens and to make sure the website kept its clean look and remained easy to navigate. Once he was happy with the results, he put together an email for Delphine with the links and a document he'd prepared to show samples of how he could customize her social media pages and newsletter headers to make her brand cohesive. Nothing was live, just sitting on his company's server waiting for feedback and approvals. He doubled checked the email's info, making sure he attached the correct document, then sent it off.

He picked up his phone and sent a text to Delphine to let her know the email was ready for her whenever she decided to take a break from work. He set his phone aside and moved on to his next to-do item. Rising from his desk, he went to the front office area.

"Helena, have we had any replies about the marketing packets we sent out to the local yacht clubs?"

"*Non*, Monsieur Chassériau."

"It's been ten days, so even slow post should have arrived by now. Why don't you take the next few days to make follow up phone calls?"

"Of course," she said, pulling out her ever-handy notepad where she kept her lists. "I can also begin prepping the next round of marketing packets, if you let me know which group of businesses you'd like me to focus on."

"Let's go with the tourism locations. I believe there's a folder with specs on the marketing drive you can use. Let me know when you have a sample packet ready. *Merci*, Helena."

His secretary nodded, jotted down a quick note, then turned to her computer to work her own brand of magic.

Jean-Paul returned to his office, determined to make his way through the slush pile of emails. He pulled up the office email program. He was able to skim over and archive several emails from the new marketing reps handling his previous clients from Nantes. It was good to see their projects moving forward. A few of the reps sent work requests for new or updated websites. He marked an email from a business college as priority, reminding himself to check his calendar to see if he could be a guest speaker later in the semester.

His phone pinged. When he swiped the screen, he saw a message from Delphine.

Wow. Fantastique! The website looks amazing. I'm going to pass the links on to my editor for his feedback, but as far as I'm concerned, it's more than I ever could have imagined. Thank you! Psst–be sure to send me an invoice.

He chuckled. He would send her an invoice, but a discounted one. The saying business wasn't personal was only partly true. He learned early in his career to not give away his services for free or else the people he helped didn't appreciate his time. But business was more than just a number on a check. Relationships were important, and he hoped things would continue to progress with Delphine. If they ended up backing off into the 'just friends' category, he'd like to be able to maintain a business relationship she would respect.

How's work going for you today? he replied.

So much better. The puzzle is finally coming together and the scenes are just flying. My brain is going to need a break soon. *hint hint*

He checked his watch and work items to complete and made a guesstimate on how long it would take to finish up before replying.

Message received. I have about two more hours of work before I can take off for the day. Would you and Hugo like to go for a walk and grab dinner? I promise to only keep you long enough for your brain to recharge.

Her answer was quickly returned.

The timing sounds about right for me, too. Just come to my apartment when you're ready. See you soon!

The next two hours crawled by, with

95

him checking the clock every ten or so minutes. He finally set a timer for twenty minutes and pushed himself to work through as much as he could before it went off. Then he continued repeating the process until he not only had his work done for the day, but had a work plan for the next day as well.

He grabbed his jacket and bid his secretary goodbye. When he arrived at Delphine's apartment building, he quickly climbed the stairs. He took a second to catch his breath, then knocked on her front door. He smiled when he heard Hugo on the other side.

The door unlatched. His breath caught. Even in yoga pants, makeup free, and a messy ponytail with a pen sticking out at the top, she was beautiful and more captivating than a galaxy of stars.

"Hi," he said, sounding like a young teenager waiting for the pretty girl to invite him in. She smiled and tilted her face up to receive *bise* kisses, her sweet fruit scent surrounding him when he pressed his cheek to hers.

"I hope you don't mind, but this is me on the average work day," she said, stepping aside and motioning for him to enter. Once the door was closed and Hugo was free, the dog sat at Jean-Paul's feet and lifted his paw in greeting.

"I quite like you in your natural habitat," he said, kneeling to shake Hugo's paw, then scratch him behind the ear.

Her eyebrows lifted up and down a few times. "Except instead of polar bears, I have Hugo to share it with. Speaking of which, Hugo, *allez*!"

Delphine handed Jean-Paul the leash, and he clipped it to Hugo's collar while she grabbed a thick sweater cardigan, then they were off. They stopped at a street vendor to purchase baguette sandwiches and cans of cola, then walked through the park until they found a bench with a pretty view of the port and the boats out on the water.

"Mmm, it feels so good to be outside," Delphine said, turning her face up to catch some rays from the soon-to-be setting sun.

Jean-Paul unwrapped his sandwich and tore off a chunk of bread to share with Hugo. "Creating is a curse, isn't it? It's a blessing when inspiration is strong. The hours slip by while I'm deep into a project, but the downside is being holed up in one place."

"*Oui*, it's true," Delphine said, taking the first bite of her sandwich. "For me, it's not talking to real people. I have so many conversations with my characters or texts with family and friends, but actually leaving my apartment and meeting friends in person, well, I tend to let that part of my life slip. Then when I come up for air, I splurge on as much interaction as I can handle before I go back into the cave." She popped open her soda can. "Speaking of cave, my editor loved the website. He asked for your contact info, so don't be surprised if he calls or emails."

"I'd really like to hear his perspective from a publishing point of view. *Merci*."

Delphine's phone buzzed. She pulled it out, and he caught a glimpse of a text message from her Papa before she swiped the screen closed.

"How is your family doing? Do you get to Switzerland very often to see them?" he asked.

She surprised him by stiffening and dropping her phone into the pocket of her cardigan. "I used to fly out once or twice a month for a long weekend, but things are complicated now." She looked down at her half-eaten sandwich and tore off a chunk for Hugo. "My Maman has Alzheimer's. It's been . . . difficult for her to have me nearby. A few months ago when I visited, she became very agitated, confusing me with her younger sister during a time when they didn't get along." When she looked up at him, the deep sadness in her eyes just about slayed him. "I thought it would be easier for her if I kept my distance."

"Has it?" Jean-Paul asked, taking her hand in his and rubbing his thumb across the top of her hand, wishing it could soothe away her pain. For someone as sweet as Delphine to gradually lose her mother in such an agonizing way seemed utterly unfair.

She gave a half-hearted shrug. "I don't know for sure. Papa has been handling everything, and he tries to always be positive about it. Lately, I've been actively trying to not think about it. It just hurts too much."

"That's not healthy either," he said. "It's a temporary coping method, at best. I know I haven't met your parents, but if you ever want to talk, I'm here for you."

She squeezed his hand, then murmured a thank you. Silence fell between them, leaving Jean-Paul unsure how to transition to another topic. Hugo hopped up and licked at their joined hands, which brought a small smile to Delphine's face.

She nodded toward the port's towers. "Have you been to the top?"

"I haven't had a chance yet," he replied, grateful to have their conversation going again.

"Do you think you're up for it? It should only take about thirty minutes."

Had he known what he was getting into, he would have rethought agreeing to the outing. "Are you sure there's an end?" he asked as they climbed what seemed to be a never-ending winding staircase to the top of the Tour de la Chain. Poor Hugo didn't last long, so Jean-Paul scooped him up. When they reached the deck area, it was just them and a few others milling around. The view of La Rochelle was incredible, but it was the oceanside with the setting sun that was stunning.

"Admit it, the view was worth the climb," she teased.

"It's stunning," he said, although he was referring to more than just the view from the tower. The way the rays of the sun glinted off her hair and bathed her skin in a warm glow took his breath away.

Delphine took out her phone, and he pulled her close as she snapped a few selfies of them together. The first few were silly, but then she leaned close and gave him a kiss on the cheek. The surprised look on his face combined with her kiss resulted in a comical photo.

"No fair," he said. "You didn't give me any warning."

"You need a warning before a girl kisses you?" she teased.

"Just for the first kiss," he replied, leaning in closer. The tip of her tongue darted out, wetting her lips as she tilted her head up in an invitation to continue. His hand slipped to the nape of her neck as he slowly lowered his head, the feel of the fast pace of her pulse against his thumb matching his own.

"Ahem," someone coughed, interrupting them when Jean-Paul was just a breath away from meeting Delphine's lips.

Delphine jumped, knocking her head into his. "Ow," she exclaimed, stepping back and rubbing the sore spot.

"*Pardon*, but the tower is closing. You need to start your descent, please," the attendant informed them.

"*Merci*," Jean-Paul said, nodding to the man. He picked up Hugo, and they made their way back down the staircase. They were almost to the bottom when his cell phone rang. The phone number was from Simply Bella.

He apologized to Delphine and answered the call, then quickly wished he hadn't.

"Jean-Paul." Angelique's voice came from the other side. "The new product lines aren't uploading to the website correctly. We are desperate for your help."

"I'm away from the office, but I'll make my way back now. I'll call you in about twenty minutes," he promised before he disconnected the call. "I'm sorry," he said, turning to Delphine. The phone call lasted long enough that they had exited the tower. "There's a problem at work and I need to get back."

"I understand. I'll just take Hugo and get back to work too."

Jean-Paul handed Hugo back to her, then hesitated, trying to figure out what to say next. Not only was their potential first kiss ruined, but so was the end of their date. "I'll see you Friday, right?"

"Absolutely. Be sure to wear steel-toed dancing shoes," she replied lightly, sending him off with a quick *bise* kiss.

As he rushed back to the office, he received a text message from his secretary.

Mme. St. Germain has arrived at the office. Said she talked with you about some emergency work that needs done. I was just getting ready to close up. What would you like me to do?

He couldn't work with Angelique distracting him. He quickly typed a reply back, begging Helena to stay until he could make a plan with Mme. St. Germain, then they could both leave at the same time. He received a thumbs up as a reply.

When he walked into the office, Helena was serving an espresso to Angelique.

"Jean-Paul," Angelique exclaimed, setting the drink aside and quickly rising from her seat. "Thank goodness you're here. I thought it would be best if we work through these issues side-by-side."

"Why don't we go into my office so we can review the situation." He motioned for Angelique to enter ahead of him, averting his eyes from the way the flowy material of her very short dress swished around her bare upper thighs. Instead, he caught his secretary's attention, widening his eyes and mouthing a silent plea for help. Thankfully she nodded, then picked up her notepad and pen and followed them into the office. Following her cue, he said, "Helena will be joining us to transcribe notes."

Angelique tried to mask her disappointed expression, but she didn't do a very good job at it.

"Let's pull up the website, then you can explain what's happening," he said. This was all work he would normally do with Perkash, who was Simply Bella's technical representative. He wondered how Perkash felt about Angelique going over his head.

"This may take quite a while. Perhaps Helena could order dinner to be delivered," Angelique suggested.

"It should only take a few minutes to identify the problem areas, then I can email you progress updates." Once the website was up, he turned the screen around so they could all view it, then pushed the mouse toward Angelique to navigate.

"I don't know which pages the issues are on," Angelique admitted after clicking through some of the links and not finding error results. "Perkash was the one who reported the problems when he was updating the stock."

If Perkash couldn't figure it out, then that worried Jean-Paul. "Let me call him and we can go from there."

Once he was connected with Perkash, it only took about ten minutes of conversation for Jean-Paul to figure out which area needed tweaking. He navigated through the back end of the website to find the code that was giving Simply Bella fits. It was a situation Perkash would have eventually figured out, but it went faster since Jean-

Paul was able to identify the specific section they needed to adjust.

"There you go, everything is back on track," Jean-Paul said, ending the conversation with Perkash and turning his attention back to Angelique.

"That was much faster than I expected. You're so talented," Angelique said, batting her eyes in a fashion that was probably meant to be alluring, but instead it came off as if she had a speck of dirt in her eyes.

Helena bit her lip as if trying to hold back a laugh before excusing herself to type up the notes from the meeting.

Jean-Paul stood and extended his hand across the desk to Angelique. "I hope your new clothing line reveal goes well."

Angelique stood in a smooth motion and placed her hand in his, not letting go. "The evening is still young. It would be nice to go out and catch up personally. No Simply Bella talk."

Her smile was flirty, but her eyes revealed a clashing mixture of pleading. Man, it made him feel like crap. They may not have grown up as best friends, but they *were* friends, and Angelique had gone out of her way to help him as a newbie in the area. At the same time, he knew her new lifestyle, and her attachment to him made him uncomfortable. How could he find a balance between their friendship and not leading her on romantically? "I appreciate the invitation, Angelique, but I had a dinner date earlier."

Her smile faltered, and she twisted her fingers around the strap of her hand bag. "Oh, I didn't realize you were involved with anyone."

He rocked back on his heels, trying to distract himself from the awkwardness of the situation. "You might remember her from the evening at the Musée d'Art. I introduced you to each other."

Her nod was slow, as if she were pulling together a picture of his date from the files of her mind. He wondered if Angelique had actually paid attention to Delphine at all that evening or if it was as Delphine suggested, that Angelique dismissed her as chopped meat. If so, that was Angelique's loss.

She shook her head. "That night was a little crazy, as we had been celebrating CeCe's birthday. I do remember running into both of you, but I honestly don't remember her name."

Out partying with her friends was just one element that could explain Angelique's bizarre behavior that evening. She didn't exactly run with a calm crowd these days.

"Delpine Baudry. We met a few weeks ago and so far, everything has been pretty *fantastique*."

"Then I'm happy for you, Jean-Paul," she said, blinking her eyes and looking away. "I should let you go. I hope you have a good remainder of the evening. Thank you for your quick problem-solving skills on the website."

He was thankful when Angelique said good evening and finally left. Was it really that simple, that all he needed to do was be clear and she'd move on? There even seemed to be a small glimmer of the real Angelique coming through. He shoved his hands in his pockets, pushing past the nagging guilt of hurting her. Instead he hoped for good things for his friend, especially if that included finding someone who helped her return to her true self.

CHAPTER ELEVEN

Friday, October 6th

IT WAS TWO O'CLOCK in the morning, and the discothèque was in full swing. The DJ pumped out his mashups, and the disco ball and flashing lights lit up the dance floor. True to her word, Viv had reserved a prime booth where Pablo and Delphine could hide from the crush of bodies doing their dance thang, but Jean-Paul was able to whisk Delphine away for several dances. He especially enjoyed getting her on the floor during the slow songs, where he was able to put all those dance classes his mother forced on him to good use. Being a strong dance lead, he could guide Delphine, adding in twirls and dips to keep her on her toes. Hearing her laughter bubble around them was the highlight of his evening.

He quickly discovered that Viv and Henrik were dance floor hounds. They knew all the moves and how to put them to good use for various tempos. Once Viv knew Jean-Paul not only enjoyed the discothèque but could also dance, she and Henrik commandeered him for all the fast songs he could handle. Delphine was content to huddle in the booth with Pablo, talking shop and plotting books.

"Viv has worn me out," he said, sliding into the booth next to Delphine. "Rescue me before she hauls me away again."

Delphine slid her hand into his. "You're not the first, my dear. Frankly, Henrik is the only person I've ever seen keep up with her."

"And even he will bow out around three-thirty or four o'clock," Pablo said before draining his wine glass. "Viv is making her way toward us. Why don't you both head over to the bar for another bottle of wine?"

"Good plan," Delphine agreed, nudging Jean-Paul out of the booth. He took her hand, and they weaved through groups towards the bar. They didn't make it far when Jean-Paul heard a familiar voice.

"Jean-Paul, *mon cheri*, how marvelous to see you here. Now the evening can truly begin," Angelique said, throwing her arm around his neck and placing a kiss, not on his cheek, but square on his lips.

From the way she clung to him, hanging

on his body as if to keep herself upright, it was obvious she had been drinking way too much. Jean-Paul nudged her back toward her group of friends gathered nearby, being rowdy and making jokes about the people on the dance floor. Angelique fit right in with her ripped jeans sitting dangerously low on her hips and a top that featured strategically placed strips of fabric over the bare essentials of her chest, not leaving much to the imagination.

"Angelique, nice to see you again." He nodded toward the familiar faces from the art gallery. "You remember my date, Delphine, I presume."

"Ah, yes, the little author." Angelique giggled in a high-pitched, very annoying manner. "I Googled her, you know." She turned to her friends, linking arms with one of the similarly dressed women. "She writes books for children. Isn't that sweet?" she asked in a decidedly not sweet fashion.

Jean-Paul bristled from Angelique's uncharacteristic rudeness. He eyed the richie rich friends she was with, knowing their presence was a major influence on her behavior. "Actually, Delphine writes best-selling science fiction novels for young adults."

"It is nice to see you again, Angelique,"

Delphine interjected, taking hold of Jean-Paul's arm. "We were on our way to get more wine before returning to our friends' table. We hope you have a fun evening."

Jean-Paul was impressed that Delphine had the sense of mind to neutralize the situation. It certainly wasn't worth the effort of trying to educate this drunken group of misfits. He took a deep breath and followed her lead, saying goodbye to the group.

But Angelique did not give up so easily. As soon as Delphine turned and took a few steps away, Angelique followed and grabbed his arm, forcing him to turn back to her. She placed her hand on his chest and leaned in close, lowering her voice to a level for just the two of them. "Jean-Paul, don't make this mistake. She's very nice, but don't you see that I love you? If you would just give us a real chance, I think you would feel the same."

Overwhelming guilt and sympathy swelled within as she pleaded her case. This was the moment he had wanted to avoid, yet here he was, facing it in a very uncomfortable and public way with her vicious friends trying to glean any tidbit they could. Jean-Paul wrapped his arm around her bare waist and pulled her a few steps away for a little more privacy before releasing her.

"Angelique, you have been a great friend to me, and not just since I moved to La Rochelle. We share many childhood memories that will last our entire lifetimes. You will always be my friend, but who is this person you've become? You used to be so confident and showed your integrity through your actions and your fashion designs. Now I see a woman who is confused and trading her self-worth for a spot with a crowd of people who hold no value in society. You are worth infinitely more than that."

She jerked away from him, hot anger pouring through her movements as she poked her finger hard into his chest. "So you don't love me because of the way I dress and the people I associate with? That's as weak as your accusations about me being confused."

"You're deliberately twisting my words around. I'm dating Delphine and am so happy with her. Think about what I just said, about your convictions. Am I wrong? Take a snapshot and look at yourself at this precise moment. Your face is hidden under a mountain of makeup, your chest is about to burst from that barely-there top, and you've had too much to drink. Your so-called friends are like hyenas, making fun of anyone they deem as less than them. I bet you a thousand euros that whatever they're texting furiously over there is gossip about the scene we're making right now. You have become the exact person you detested in *lycee* and university." He took a deep breath to calm his tone before continuing. "I do care for you, Angelique. Enough that I want to see you have the future you always talked about." He motioned from her head to toe. "This is not it."

Angelique stepped back, opening and closing her mouth like a fish searching for air. Someone snapped a picture, the bright multi-layered flash blinding him. Jean-Paul blinked several times before all the spots cleared from his vision, only to capture a brief glimpse of Angelique's back as she disappeared into the crowd. He swore softly, disappointed with the change in their friendship.

He turned, anxious to find Delphine. He discovered her a few paces away, wide-eyed and glued to her spot as people surged around her this way and that. Not wanting to be the subject of any more drama, he took her hand and led her the remainder of the way to the bar, quickly placing an order for a bottle of red and a bottle of white.

"You picked me," Delphine said when he

turned to face her again. "She's super model gorgeous and I'm just messy, clutzy me."

He cupped her face with his hands and dropped a quick kiss on the corner of her mouth. "Earth to Delphine . . . I plan to always choose you."

*****

"Hey, sleepy head, we're here," Jean-Paul whispered to her, but all she wanted to do was snuggle in closer and breathe in the scent of his cologne. Mmm, that was the smell of happy dreams filled with meadows and tantalizing kisses.

Something sharp pressed into her side, making her eyes fly open.

"Wakey, wakey, Delphine." Henrik pressed his elbow into her side again. "Let's get a move on. If I'm not in bed before the sun comes up, then I just can't get to sleep."

"Okay," she slurred. "I'm awake." She looked up at Jean-Paul and smiled. "Or at least partly awake," she said, closing her eyes and putting her head on his shoulder again.

"Oh lordy, that girl isn't going to make it up to her apartment before she's back to sleep again. Go get her inside, then hurry back, Jean-Paul."

The car door opened, and she tumbled to the car seat when Jean-Paul slid out. She stuck her tongue out at her friends, who were laughing at her expense, then slid across the seat to join Jean-Paul on the sidewalk.

The chilled early morning air bit through her cardigan as he took her hand and led her into her building. "Just follow me and take care to not trip on the stairs."

"Okie dokie," she said, allowing him to lead her along. And really, the view of Jean-Paul from behind was not an ounce short of A+. The man could talk science, he got her whole nutty writers brain, and he could dance. He could even make it look like she could sort of dance. That was quite the feat in itself. And he liked her. Not that crazy Angelique. Her, Delphine Baudry, geeky chick who could craft words on paper but stumble over them in real life. Sigh. She almost felt like she was living in an alternate reality. She wanted to stay there forever if it meant being with him.

"Oops," she said, giggling when she bumped into him from behind. Oh, look, they were at her apartment door. That took a lot less time than she remembered. Or maybe it was just her sleepy brain malfunctioning.

Jean-Paul turned so that she was leaning against the apartment door. He stepped closer and wrapped his arms around her waist. "You're pretty cute when you're sleepy."

Ooh, and she loved this. Her sleepy brain = less filters and somehow the words, "Are you going to kiss me goodnight?" slipped out of her mouth.

His lips twitched into a cute lopsided smile. One hand came up and wrapped some loose curls around a finger. "I love your curls."

Her curls? Was he trying to change the subject? Dodge the end-of-the-date kiss? A little wedge of hurt crept in.

He let the curls slide free from his finger, then cupped the side of her face with his hand, his thumb brushing over her cheek. Her eyes drifted closed as he leaned down and placed a sweet kiss on one cheek, then on the other. His lips lingered on the last kiss. She inhaled as she felt the skin of his cheek brush against hers, the combination of his cologne and stubble from his five o'clock shadow creating crazy reactions all over her body. Then his lips landed on the arch of her neck, nibbling where her pulse beat like the hectic tempo from the discothèque.

116

Beep-Beep-Be-Be-Beep!

The moan that escaped wasn't one of pleasure, but one of annoyance for her friends honking their car horn. At least Jean-Paul's groan accompanied hers. They both held very still as they steadied their breathing.

Jean-Paul pulled back, regret on his face. "Do you have your keys?"

Her keys? Oh, for the door. She handed them to him. She heard Hugo running toward the door at the sound of the lock turning.

"Have sweet dreams," he said, then he dropped a kiss on the tip of her nose before opening the door and nudging her safely inside, depositing the keys in her hand.

"Goodnight," she said, sad for the evening to end. She locked the door and listened as his footsteps clomped down the stairs until they faded away. Everything inside of her wished she could call him back and make time come to a halt so they could just be together. Most of all, she hoped that her heart, which had completely tumbled into love, would be safe in his hands.

CHAPTER TWELVE

Monday, October 9th

DELPHINE DRAGGED HER WEARY BODY into a sitting position at the edge of her bed Monday morning. She glared at the clock, noting that it was already after nine and she had lost at least an hour of productivity. She tried to calculate how to catch up on her work, then collapsed back onto the bed. Who was she kidding? After sleeping most of the weekend, she still wasn't completely recovered from her late night at the discothèque. She was a pathetic excuse for a party girl.

Still, a smile tugged at her lips as she closed her eyes and remembered dancing with Jean-Paul. The touch of his hand on her lower back, sending tingles along her spine. How their gazes came back to each other like magnets when he twirled her around. The tug and pull of attraction, like chemicals mixing in a beaker. Bubbling, simmering, just waiting for the right combination of energy and matter to lead to the grand finale.

She sighed. All the ingredients were there and should have culminated in their first kiss. Blast her friends for interrupting what would have been a beautiful moment.

Hugo jumped onto the bed and licked Delphine's hand, reminding her of his presence and need for his morning walk. "All right, I'm getting up. Just give me a minute to put on shoes."

She changed into yoga pants and a sweater, then slipped her feet into some shoes. Hugo pranced in excitement as she clipped his leash on. The brisk morning air did a fine job of waking Delphine up as they walked down the block to the neighborhood park. She pulled out her phone to check her messages and smiled when she discovered one that Jean-Paul sent earlier in the morning.

I'm on the train, heading for Bordeaux to meet with your publisher about their online marketing and author websites. Wish me luck! Psst–have you recovered yet, sleepy head?

She smiled, happy that Michel contacted

Jean-Paul to set up a slew of meetings over the next few days. It would be a wonderful boost for Jean-Paul's business. She quickly typed a reply.

Still sluggish, but Hugo is relentless. Walking to the park now. Hoping it will help my brain wake up so I can get some productive editing done. Good luck today! Looking forward to hearing all about it.

As soon as they were near a grassy area, Hugo ran for the nearest bush. Delphine shifted her weight from one foot to the other, trying to keep warm until he returned to complete their walk. *Autumn is certainly in full swing*, she thought, taking in the changing color of leaves and the blooming Black-eyed Susans and mums in the flower beds. It was a beautiful time of year. She stopped in a small alcove to do some stretching, then she and Hugo headed back toward home.

As she came up the stairs to her apartment, her phone rang. The screen displayed her father's name, and she swiped the screen to answer. "*Bonjour*, Papa. How are you?" She placed the phone in the crook of her neck as she unlocked the door.

Her father's voice sounded tired and cracked when he said her name. "Delphine, *ma petite.* We need to talk."

No good conversation ever started out with the words 'we need to talk.' Delphine sank onto the couch as he delivered news about her Maman.

"I had just gotten out of the shower and was getting dressed when I realized the house was too quiet. Apparently, she decided to go outside, but the rain made the steps slick and she took a tumble. I discovered her lying on the ground in the courtyard."

"Oh no," Delphine gasped, horrified as she imagined her Maman losing her balance and crashing down the stone steps, landing on the equally hard paved courtyard. All sorts of horrid scenarios ran through her mind at lightning speed. Was she bleeding? Had she injured her head, broken any bones, or any other of the myriad injuries older generations were prone to? How long had she been lying there in the cold rain? "Is she okay?"

"She has some nasty bruises and they've admitted her for observation. Her confusion about where she is and why, combined with the constant changing of nurses and doctors, has been problematic to figure out if they're signs of a concussion or symptoms from the Alzheimer's."

Her eyes stung and her lips quivered as she tried to hold back the firestorm of emotions rushing through her. "Oh, Papa, I'm so sorry. Let me come help. Give me a few hours and I can either be on a train or a flight." She stood, making her way to her bedroom, intent on packing, her mind already creating a to-do list of items to take care so she could leave right away.

"*Ma petite*, no," her papa said. "It would be better to wait until your Maman is out of the hospital. I think she will be less confused when she has returned home."

Even knowing her father spoke the truth, being asked to wait felt like a dagger piercing her heart. All she wanted was to be by her Maman's side, to soothe and comfort her. It was crushing to realize in an emergency situation, her presence would have the opposite effect.

"Right now, the plan is to keep her overnight for observation. So perhaps Wednesday or Thursday?" he suggested.

"Very well. I will look into train tickets and airfare," she said, trying not to sound discouraged. She certainly didn't want to put more on her papa's shoulders.

"I will keep you updated. Try not to worry too much, okay?"

They both knew his request was

pointless, but she murmured her agreement nonetheless.

"It will be good to see you, Delphine. *Je t'aime.*"

"I love you, too, Papa," she said before disconnecting their call. Her hand dropped to her side, still clutching the phone while she remained frozen in her bedroom doorway. The desire to curl up in her bed and have a good cry was so strong, she nearly gave in to it. The only thing stopping her was knowing her Maman would want her to stay strong. But even strong women cried, she thought, wiping at her wet cheeks.

She needed to make a list and prioritize what needed to be done. Yes, she needed a plan. She grabbed a pen and notepad off her desk, then settled into the overstuffed chair beside the window, hoping the sunlight might work a little magic on her downhearted spirit. She put her pen to the paper and the list began. And grew and grew. She reviewed the many to-do items and divided it into more realistic Today, Tomorrow, and Next Week lists. If she planned to leave Wednesday, she needed to make the most of today and Tuesday. She wanted to be solely focused on her family while she was in Switzerland. The new lists refined the next week into more manageable tasks while helping her to also feel a bit more in control as well.

The next few days were hectic as Delphine bounced back and forth between the first full read-through and edit of her manuscript, talking with her papa, booking her train tickets, and packing for both her and Hugo. She missed Jean-Paul and wished he wasn't in Bordeaux. She was grateful for the success he was having at his meetings, but she yearned for the simple comfort of putting her head on his shoulder.

Even though they were both running in different directions, Jean-Paul let her know she was at the forefront of his thoughts by sending messengers with surprises each day. Monday it had been a bouquet of printer ink cartridges accompanied with a fun set of colored pens and sticky notes to help her jump-kick her editing week. Tuesday afternoon he sent a variety of chocolate for her and doggie treats for Hugo for their trip. The gifts left her feeling loved, but also deepened her longing to see him.

*****

Wednesday, October 11th

Delphine rushed through the train

124

station Wednesday morning. Her stupid taxi had arrived late to pick her and Hugo up, then SHE had to fight her way through a large group of tourists crowding the entry into the station. She glanced at the departure list and times on the wall, noting that she had fifteen minutes before her train departed.

The platform she needed was just ahead. She drew in a deep breath, grateful she didn't need to make a full-out run for the train. The combination of pulling her suitcase and hoisting Hugo in his carry bag was awkward, to say the least, but she could manage for just a few more minutes.

"Delphine!"

She turned when someone called her name, sure it was meant for someone else. Then she stumbled and froze in the middle of the walkway. Jean-Paul navigated through the crowd, rushing towards her, a duffle bag swinging awkwardly over one shoulder. She blinked, sure she must be seeing things. He was stuck in Bordeaux until that evening, with one more day of meetings. How could he be here?

His breath came out in hard pants when he stopped before her. He dropped his bags at his feet before pulling her into a hug. "I couldn't let you go to Switzerland without seeing you first."

Hot tears stung her eyes as she wrapped her arms around his shoulders, her fingers gripping the fleece material of his jacket. "I can't believe you're here," she said, her head buried into his shoulder as he held her tight while Hugo barked up a storm from inside his bag.

Jean-Paul gave her another slight squeeze, then stepped back, his hands moving to her shoulders. "I wasn't sure I was going to make it." His eyes darted up to the clock, then back to her. "We need to hurry to get you to the train."

He slung his bag over his shoulder, then grabbed her suitcase in one hand and clasped her hand with the other. When they reached the platform, he signaled for a porter and tipped him to take care of her luggage for the trip.

"I was—" she started, but he shushed her.

"We only have a minute. Let's not waste it talking about luggage," he said. He lifted her hand and kissed the inside of her palm. "I know you're terrified to make this trip. There are a lot of unknowns lying ahead."

She blinked, trying to ward off prickling warning at the back of her eyes. Instead she bit her lip hard, hoping to not turn into a puddle of mush.

126

He stepped in close and cupped her face with both hands. "It's okay to be scared, Delphine. Courage doesn't mean no fear. It means you keep moving forward and facing the challenge anyway. You can do this. I have faith in you."

A sob escaped. Those words. How did he know she needed them? His thumbs swiped at the tears streaking down her cheeks. She opened her mouth to say something, but couldn't form any words.

"It's okay. I know," he said. Then he kissed both her cheeks. The conductor's call for final passengers echoed down the platform. "It's time. The train is going to leave." He helped her up the steps to board the train. "Be brave," he said in a final parting.

Delphine pushed her way onto the train car, maneuvering Hugo's bag down the narrow aisle, then sat in a seat at a window nearest to Jean-Paul. She pressed her palm against the cool glass and mouthed '*Merci*' as the train lurched forward, taking her away from the man she needed and toward the journey she wasn't sure she was ready to face.

*****

"*Ma petite*, it is so good to see your lovely face," Papa said as he greeted Delphine late Wednesday evening. He pulled her into an awkward hug, patting her shoulder before stepping back. "Come," he said, ushering her inside. "Your Maman is already in bed, but you might pop in to say goodnight."

Delphine nodded, then swallowed past the lump. *Be brave*, she reminded herself. Perhaps her Maman would be doing better now that she was home.

She entered the dimly lit room, which had remained much the same since they moved here during her teen years. She remembered many nights entering her parents' bedroom to check in after late night evening activities and finding her Maman just as she was now, snuggled up in bed with the quilt pulled up to her shoulders, a word search and pen in hand.

Maman looked up when she entered the room, and her pale green eyes brightened. "Oh, my dear, I'm so happy to see you!"

Delphine's heart skipped a beat. Perhaps this trip was the miracle she needed, a bit of time to talk with her Maman. Gratitude for this moment swelled inside, making her heart feel as if it would burst. She moved quickly to the bed and set her hand on her Maman's leg. "You are looking so much better, Maman."

Maman's face twitched, and confusion clouded her gaze. "Are you feeling okay, Valérie?" She reached out and patted Delphine's hand where it rested.

Reality crashed around Delphine, like an asteroid striking the earth and leaving a crater the size of Mount Everest in its wake. She tried to make her quivering lips form a smile, but she was sure she failed miserably. "I'm just tired. It's been a long day of traveling, but I'm so happy to be here with you now. Perhaps I'll leave you to your word search so I can finish my unpacking."

"That seems sensible, dear," Maman said, patting her hand once more.

Delphine dropped a *bise* kiss on her Maman's cheek and whispered a quick, "*Je t'aime*." Then she made a hasty retreat to her bedroom. She wasn't ready to confront her mother's illness. She let the tears freely fall. Tomorrow would be soon enough to put on her brave armor.

After getting Hugo settled and herself unpacked, she let Hugo out into the backyard for a bit of fresh air and joined her father in the kitchen.

"Your timing is just right," he said, pouring his homemade *chocolat chaud* into large white bowls and setting a plate of sliced brioche on the table.

"*Merci*," she said, taking a seat across from him. She broke off a piece of brioche, dipped it into the *chocolat chaud*, then popped it into her mouth. Sweetness burst across her taste buds, reviving memories of all the mornings her family shared this simple breakfast together. "How is Maman truly doing?" she asked, then lifted the bowl to sip some cocoa.

The round slump of his shoulders matched the deep, heavy exhale that escaped as Papa tapped the side of the bowl with his fingertips. "She was lucky, *ma petite*. Her injuries could have been much worse."

She covered his hand with her own, noticing for the first time the loose, dry skin that bunched up into wrinkles beneath her fingers. A contrast from his once strong, firm hands. "But she is okay. We have that to be grateful for."

"This time," he responded, before going to the hutch and retrieving something from a drawer. He set a pile of pamphlets on the table when he returned.

"What are these?" she asked, spreading them out on the the table. Words like respite, professional, and facilities jumped out at her. She met her father's concerned expression with one of her own.

130

"The doctors recommended that we begin to consider care facilities," he said.

"You would send Maman away?" Delphine shoved the pamphlets away, unable to believe he would do such a thing.

He carefully restacked the pamphlets and held them in his hands, his eyes not leaving the top one. "There will come a time when I won't be able to take care of her, Delphine. The doctors recommend making a plan before that time comes."

"How can we abandon her, Papa?" she asked with a grief-stricken voice. "How can we just drop her off, then drive away to live our normal lives?" She dropped her head into her hands. She wasn't ready for this conversation, for this stage of her mother's horrible illness.

"I have been battling with the same questions for many months. There is one option I'd like you to consider." He set the top pamphlet on the table and slid it across to her. "It is a village for families who have loved ones with memory loss. It's like any other small village; it has a doctor's office, grocery store, homes, and parks. But everyone who works there is trained to care for and help people with memory loss. Rather than a care center where your mother would be left behind, I could move

131

here with her. We could live in a true community, one that understands and takes care of each other."

She hesitantly pulled the pamphlet toward her with her fingertips, but couldn't force herself to open it. Her Papa's warm hand covered hers this time, sending a measure of comfort.

"Look it over while you're here, *ma petite*. I won't make this decision without you."

She nodded, then bid him goodnight, taking the pamphlet with her. When she and Hugo were settled for the night, she looked at the pamphlet setting on the side table.

Be brave, Delphine.

She snatched it up and opened it quickly before she lost her nerve. There were pictures of various shops and people in the community. They looked happy, content even. Could that be possible for her mother? Or would the new location only serve to confuse her even more? She continued reading about the trained professionals who worked and some who even lived in the community—from police officers to medical professionals to the clerks at the grocery store. Each of them knew how to interact with and care for the people who lived in their small community. She set the pamphlet back on the side table, then readjusted her position in bed, wondering about possibilities for her parents' futures.

CHAPTER THIRTEEN

Tuesday, October 17th

TUESDAY MORNING, Delphine woke up in the comfort of her own bed. Hugo was snuggled up at her side, his blankets bunched up around him like a warm cocoon.

The trip to Switzerland had been difficult, but it also revealed some things she missed before. While she had previously focused on how difficult her mother's illness was, what she discovered on this visit was how much her father valued his relationship with Delphine at this point in their lives. Their conversations were much more meaningful, and they even spent time playing chess and actually laughing together as they shared favorite family memories. They also spent some time discussing the future and even set a date to tour the community Papa was considering.

It was an unexpected turn of events, but one that soothed the ache she felt for her Maman. And in a way, a blessing for both her and Papa.

But now she was back in La Rochelle. She needed to pull out the to-do list of items she pushed off to this week and refocus. Plus, she was anxious to see Jean-Paul, to tell him how much his support meant. They had texted while she was gone, but she craved some face-to-face time.

She dived into her morning routine, planning out her day. As she finished breakfast, the doorbell rang. She looked through the peephole and saw a messenger with flowers on her doorstep. After accepting them, she closed the door and set the flowers on the desk in the living room. She stepped back to admire the beautiful autumn colors bursting from the blooms. She slipped her thumb under the envelope and opened the card.

Welcome home.
XOXO - JP

She couldn't help but smile with delight as she dialed his number.

"*Bonjour*," he said, answering the call.

"I just received the most gorgeous
135

delivery of flowers. *Merci beaucoup*," she said, adjusting the flowers to the perfect spot so she could view them while she worked throughout the morning.

"Mmm, it's so good to hear your voice," he said.

His words sent a fluttering feeling throughout Delphine, making her grip the phone as if it could substitute for a hug. "Ditto," she replied.

"I have a proposition for you," Jean-Paul said.

"What is it?" she asked, swaying from side to side and feeling all flirty.

"Would you like to meet at our cafe for *chocolat chaud* at four o'clock this afternoon?"

She wanted to shout yes! Instead she reigned her enthusiasm in. "I would love to."

"Perfect. I can't wait to see you," he said before ending the call.

Delphine spun in circles, her arms open wide. Hugo yipped and jumped around, joining in her jubilee. She was going to see Jean-Paul in seven hours! Just seven more hours!

She crashed into the couch and plopped down, laughing when Hugo jumped up, licking her face and yipping at her silly game. She took a deep breath as she calmed down, looked at the clock, and began the countdown.

How in the world would she survive the next seven hours?

*****

Fleurette greeted Delphine and Hugo when they arrived at the café later that afternoon. Since Jean-Paul wasn't there yet, Delphine grabbed a table and ordered a *chocolat chaud*. Once she was seated, Hugo circled, then settled with his front paws over one of her feet.

"Would you like a treat?" Delphine asked, pulling out a doggie treat and offering it to Hugo, which of course the spoiled little guy was happy to receive.

Delphine rested her elbow on the table, admiring the changes the mid-October season had brought to the plaza since that fateful day almost a month ago when she first met Jean-Paul. The sea breezes had an underlying cooler tone, making her grateful for her cozy cardigan. The trees' leaves were turning fiery shades of yellows, oranges, and reds, making even the glow of the sun's rays seem filled with more warmth. Autumn was an enchanting season.

"It's a beautiful day, is it not?" Fleurette asked as she set the cup and saucer on the café table.

"It really is," Delphine replied. "I need to soak in as many of them as possible before the season changes and everything moves inside for the winter."

"*Oui*, our manager has already scheduled to close the patio in about three, maybe four more weeks. How is your latest book coming along?"

Delphine smiled. She had spent a lot of time writing at this café over the past few years and had developed a wonderful relationships with most of the staff. "I'm almost done with the first round of edits, so it's moving along. Although this isn't a work visit. I'm meeting a friend soon."

"*Bien*," Fleurette said, with a nod of her head. "I will let you enjoy your drink and will check back on you in a few minutes. Oh, before I go, I was asked to deliver this to you." Fleurette pulled a little white envelope from her apron.

Delphine hesitantly took it. "What is it?"

"I guess you'll have to read it to find out," Fleurette said, repeating a phrase Delphine often said when asked questions about her books. "Oh, the bill has already been taken care of." The pretty waitress winked before leaving.

Delphine slid her hand over the smooth

138

envelope, noting the high quality of the paper. Did Jean-Paul realize he wasn't going to be able to meet her and sent a note to break the news? Wouldn't he have just sent a text, though? She turned the letter over in her hand, not wanting to open, worried about what was inside.

Hugo yipped from his spot below. Well, if it was bad news, at least she had him to comfort her. She broke the seal and pulled out a sheet of thick paper. She recognized Jean-Paul's handwriting, then focused on the actual words.

Delphine,

It's been four weeks since our first meeting. It seems like the right time for a little adventure. Location #1 - the café where we had our first conversation. Your next stop–the record shop.

See you soon!

Jean-Paul

A wave of relief washed over her. She could handle this. She quickly read over the note again, a smile tugging at her lips. It looked like a scavenger hunt of sorts. She quickly drank her *chocolat chaud*, then set the cup and saucer aside. "I have a feeling we're bound for a little adventure, Hugo."

He jumped to his feet, tail wagging and

ready to explore. His enthusiasm matched her own as she wondered what Jean-Paul had schemed up.

"Have fun," Fleurette called from where she was greeting another customer.

Delphine waved, then set off for the flea market, keeping an eye out and trying to spot Jean-Paul. Was he watching her progress from afar, or had he planted all the clues in advance and was simply waiting for her at the final destination?

She arrived at the vinyl record booth, not sure how to go about searching for the next clue. She scanned the tables, looking for an envelope tucked under the corner of one of the boxes, but didn't find anything.

"Can I help you?" A middle-aged man sporting a Nirvana concert shirt approached her from the other side of the table.

"I'm not sure. I'm looking for something a friend may have left behind." She felt silly. How did she explain that an adult was on a scavenger hunt?

"You know, I've heard that girls just want to have fun. Does that help?"

Delphine's eyes widened, remembering the conversation with Jean-Paul about the various records they'd discovered. "Cyndi Lauper!"

She went to the bin and sorted through

140

until she found the album. She lifted it out, then turned it around and found an envelope taped to the back. She gently peeled it off, making sure not to damage the album cover.

"Mademoiselle, may I?" The vendor produced a canvas bag and tucked the record inside before offering it to her. "It was purchased for you."

"Really? Thank you," she said, filled with delight.

"Enjoy the rest of your day," the vendor said before turning his attention to a group of college students browsing the record collections.

Delphine stepped out of the booth, then walked out of the crowd of vendors to a bench where she could sit and read the next clue.

Delphine -
Michael Jackson's Thriller may not be for you, but there's another location where the view is more than thrilling–it's stunning.
See you soon!
Jean-Paul

Along the bottom of the note, he sketched the skyline of the port. During their trip to the tower, Jean-Paul said the view was stunning. That must be the next destination. "*Allez*, Hugo," she said, and they set off. When they arrived, she looked at all the stairs and knew poor Hugo's legs must be getting tired with all their exploring. She bent and picked him up, then began the ascent. Every step closer had her wondering if Jean-Paul would be there to meet her. Perhaps to recreate their almost first kiss. Anticipation filled her like bubbles fizzing and overflowing from a soda can that had been all shaken up.

She didn't see Jean-Paul when she emerged onto the tower's deck, so she circled around, from city-side to ocean-view side. And there, on one of the tower ledges, was a small green box topped with a white envelope with her name scrawled across the front. It was strange how disappointment could well up, yet at the same time, an even more intense sense of yearning to reunite with Jean-Paul pulled at her. She peeled off the envelope, impatient to see what the next clue was.

Delphine -
Time for a short break–I'm sure Hugo's paws will appreciate it. Enjoy the view before moving on to the final destination . . . where our journey first crossed paths.

See you soon!
Jean-Paul

She lifted the top of the box, then peeked in and found a postcard of the tower, a disposable bowl, a bottle of water, some doggie treats for Hugo, and a bag of dried mixed fruit for her. Part of her just wanted to keep going, but looking down at Hugo, she knew Jean-Paul was right. The little guy needed a bit of a break. She set the bowl on the deck and poured a little water inside. Hugo happily lapped it up. She munched on her own treats and sipped on water while she looked out over the ocean, reflecting on the last time she and Jean-Paul were here.

Over the past few weeks, she had shared some of her favorite spots in La Rochelle with Jean-Paul, each time also opening up about different aspects of her life. Their conversations and time together continued to strengthen their friendship, bringing him much closer to her than any other man had come. Part of that realization was nerve-wracking, but it was over-shadowed by her desire to grow closer to Jean-Paul, to discover what their next steps could be together. Feeling the urge to reach the final destination, she cleaned up their snacks, threw away the trash, and stowed the postcard and envelope with the other items in the canvas bag before picking up Hugo.

One more stop to meet the man she had very much given her heart to.

*****

Jean-Paul paced in another circle around the fountain, his heart beating hard against his chest as he waited for his first glimpse of Delphine. He had fun using his sneaky skills to set up each stop of the scavenger hunt, staying only about fifteen minutes ahead of her to make sure the plans were all in place. This last stop was tricky because he had no way of knowing how long she would linger at the tower. The waiting was driving him crazy.

He shifted the velvet bag full of coins from hand to hand, the clinking sound providing some distraction from constantly searching the faces nearby. Finally, there she was, with Hugo leading the way across the plaza toward where he stood. His feet suddenly glued themselves to the cobblestones, unable to move even though all he wanted was to rush forward and pull her close.

"*Bonjour*," Delphine said, a pretty flush rising on her face as she lifted to her toes to

144

place a kiss on his cheek. Hugo jumped up on his leg, demanding his own greeting as well.

He wrapped one hand around her waist, keeping her close, breathing in the light scent of her cherry-vanilla lotion. "I missed you," he admitted. "Six days apart is way too long."

"Agreed," she said, resting against him in a light embrace for a moment before pulling back. "Hugo and I had a fun adventure with your scavenger hunt."

With all the stress of her deadlines and the trip to see her parents, he was relieved to see some lightheartedness in her expression. He felt a rush of pride that he helped to put it there. Now, on to what he hoped was a turning point for them.

"I'm glad you enjoyed it." He reached down and patted Hugo's head to appease him before continuing. "So, it's been almost a month since we met right here, two strangers making wishes for their careers. Thankfully the Fairy Godmother over the wishing fountain stepped in and intertwined our paths."

Delphine smiled. "Either I'm rubbing off on you, or you have a gift for words I didn't know about."

He reached up and tucked her silky hair

behind her ear, his thumb caressing her cheek before dropping to capture her hand in his. "Oh, it's definitely you."

"Good, I like that," she said, her smile making crinkles around her eyes, happiness radiating from her.

He lifted his other hand with the bag of coins, opened it, and pulled out just one. "There's this old saying that if you wish for true love with your back to the fountain and toss the coin over your shoulder, your wish will be granted."

He transferred the bag of coins from his hand to hers, placing her free hand over the top so the bag was securely in her possession. "We were brought together by wishes that had nothing to do with romance, but the way I feel about you has my heart all wrapped up and labeled with a tag that has your name on it. So here's my wish." He held up the coin. "I wish for enough time together that I can grant you all the wishes you desire, and when that bag is empty, I hope we'll choose to fulfill each other's wishes forever more."

Delphine's eyes softened as he kissed the coin, then closed his eyes and tossed it over his shoulder to the fountain behind him. He opened just one eye to see Delphine tilted to the side, watching the coin's journey. "Please tell me it actually landed in the fountain," he said.

Delphine giggled, then looked back at him. "The fountain's Fairy Godmother has successfully received your wish."

"Whew," he said, pretending to wipe sweat from his brow, waiting for her reaction. He knew it was all rather corny, but the combination of corny and geeky seemed to be part of what drew them together.

Delphine hefted the coins in her hand. "Any wish I desire?"

"Anything," he said, hoping his promise would prove to always be true.

Her smile turned devilish, her hand coming up to caress his jaw line. "Even a first kiss from the man I've fallen in love with?"

His breath caught, joy swelling like an explosion of atoms when stars are born in outer-space. "I would be happy to grant that wish for the woman I love."

He brought both hands up to cradle her face, her long blonde curls moving with the gentle breeze. He dipped his head and captured her lips with his, tender and lingering. She melted into him, her hand slipping to the back of his head and sinking into his hair, turning their kiss from sweet to passionate before he remembered they were in a public place and reined himself back in. He softened the kiss before breaking it and resting his forehead against hers. He took her hand holding the bag of coins and rested it against his chest.

"Being with you is the best wish come true," he said, with a perfect hope for their future together.

DISCOVER THE
INDULGENCE ROW SERIES

SWEET CONFECTIONS

2015 RONE Award for
Best Contemporary Sweet Romance

According to Rachel Marconi chocolate heals all wounds. That and throwing darts at pictures of her ex-boyfriend. Burned by yet another bad relationship, Rachel decides to reprioritize her life, putting her dream to compete on a Food Network Challenge on the top of her list and dating at the bottom crossed out in red sharpie.

Cue in Graydon Green, a former pro hockey player turned restaurant owner. After a lot of persistent and humorous teasing, he finally convinces Rachel to commit to a date. Just when things begin to warm up, threatening notes directed at Rachel arrive. When her bakery is vandalized, Graydon's protective streak goes on red alert. Is it her obsessive ex-boyfriend stalking her? Or maybe a challenger trying to sabotage the competition?

Either way, Rachel is definitely going to need more chocolate - perhaps drizzled over ice cream and devil's food cake.

SWEET CONFECTIONS

CHAPTER ONE PREVIEW

LIFE AS A SINGLE CHICK SUCKED. Well, not all of it. Rachel loved designing cakes at the upscale bakery she co-owned with her best friend. Kicking butt at local and state cake competitions made work all the sweeter. No, there were lots of great elements about life in general, but the search for The Guy was exhausting. Was it really too much for a girl to ask for interesting conversation not centered around sports, a guy who laughed at corny jokes—possibly even himself at times—and a kiss with some zing? Major zing would be most appreciated.

She'd had visions of left-handed sparkle in the not-so-distant future with Nico Giambiasi. Instead she sat at Brisket and Noodles, one of Kansas City's popular BBQ restaurants, decked out in her favorite clingy jeans, an emerald top that contrasted nicely with her deep red hair and killer heels, trying to absorb the bomb her boyfriend just dropped.

"Are you serious? You're married?" Rachel pushed her hair back over her shoulder, although she was tempted to wrap it around her fingers and pull hard to see if this conversation was real or just a horrible dream.

"It's not what you think, darling." Nico reached across the table, but she moved her hands to her lap.

"Really? We've been dating for three months! What am I supposed to think?" She searched his face for signs of something she must have missed, but all she saw were dark good looks. She leaned back in the seat and placed a hand over her stomach, trying to hold back the bubble of hysterical laughter gathering within. Dimly, she heard him talking, but couldn't focus on the words. How could this be true? Sure he left for extended trips, often flying back to Italy where the company he worked for was based. But married? Never in a thousand million years would she have guessed he was spoken for in a very permanent way. Had all the time they spent together really been one big tangled web of lies? There should be a cell phone app that monitors your social calendar and sends a flashing neon text message after ten dates with a reminder that it's probably time to apply the one thing the males species ever got right—the Boy Scout motto. 'Be Prepared' and locate the nearest emergency exit.

Then she heard something that made her sit up straight. "Stop. Say that again." She shook her head. She couldn't have possibly heard him right.

"I said if it weren't for the kids, I would have left Denita long before I met you."

"Your kids?" she squeaked. The image of a little boy covered in dust and dirt and a sweet girl holding her baby doll with no daddy to play with popped into her head. Nico was lucky the table wasn't preset with sharp knives. The jerk. She leaned forward and lowered her voice. "You make me sick." She pushed back from the table and stood to leave, but he grabbed her arm and pulled her close.

"You need to listen, Rachel." Anger sharpened his features. Her heart pounded against her chest as she attempted to step away but he pulled her closer still. "Sit down. I'm not finished yet."

She reached for a glass of water, intending to throw it in his face, but he took the goblet from her. "Please, that is so cliché."

Her nails bit into the palm of her hand,

then the next thing she knew, her fist connected with his nose. Pain shot up her forearm, all the way to her elbow. Holy mackerel. She had never hit anyone before, but thankfully her brothers made her learn how to do it properly.

Nico gasped and released her, bending over to cover his face. She took the opportunity to snatch her purse and get away, quickly weaving between the tables toward the front of the restaurant. Well, Rachel, she thought, this is what you get for meeting people online. Didn't Mom tell you there were a bunch of loonies out there? But did you listen? Of course not. As she neared the foyer, Nico yanked her around to face him. A trickle of blood ran down from his nose. A wave of queasiness washed over her when he reached up and wiped it with the back of his hand. He looked at the smeared blood, then shoved his hand into his pocket before returning his attention to her.

"Where do you think you're going? You came with me and you'll leave with me." People waiting to be seated stopped talking and stared at the drama unfolding before them.

"Let go of me, Nico. You're causing a scene," she said quietly. Instead, his hand tightened on her arm, making her wince.

What was he doing? He had always been charming and sweet—until tonight. Was it all a masquerade?

"Excuse me, but I believe the lady asked you to let her go."

The deep voice came from over her shoulder. Nico glanced up and his eyes widened, then narrowed. He slowly released her arm.

Rachel automatically stepped away, but bumped into a solid chest. She moved to the side and looked up . . . and up.

Beside her stood one of the tallest men she'd ever seen. She was an average girl who could hit 5'8" with the right heels on, but still, her head barely came to the middle of his chest. He turned and blocked Nico from her.

"Are you okay, miss?" he asked in an unexpectedly gentle voice. She forced herself to nod, but couldn't seem to make her vocal cords work. He studied her for a moment, then gave a return nod. When he turned around, she saw Nico's face harden with resentment and a shiver ran down her spine.

"Rachel," Nico said tightly. "This is enough. I'm taking you home, now."

"I believe she's changed her mind. You can say goodnight." Her rescuer motioned to the front door.

Nico looked as if he might push the issue, but instead turned away and pulled his coat on. "I'll call you tomorrow."

"Don't." She couldn't stand the thought of being near him. If she didn't get away from him soon, her roiling stomach would force her to the nearest restroom or trash can.

"I'll call you tomorrow," he repeated, then shoved the door open and stormed out.

Married. He's married, married, married.

"Excuse me," the man said, stepping to her side. "Perhaps you'd like to come into the office while you wait for a cab?"

Rachel tightened her grip on her purse, trying unsuccessfully to quiet the jumbled confusion in her head. "Yes, thank you. I'd appreciate that."

"Max, please call a cab and let me know when it arrives."

The restaurant host gave a slight nod in acknowledgment, then she followed the man down a short hallway and into a masculine office. Simple black framed pictures of hockey players and teams lined the wall behind the desk. He motioned to the black leather couch sitting in front of a large mahogany desk. "Please sit while I get you a drink."

She sank into the soft, buttery leather and closed her eyes, concentrating, searching for the calm she needed to make it home before falling apart. She could keep herself together. She would keep herself together. She opened her eyes to find the manager standing before her with a glass of ice water. She'd noticed his height, but didn't realize how big he really was. Medium brown hair fell forward onto his forehead, his shoulders were wide and everything else was all muscle. The combination of being in the small office and him standing near made her claustrophobic. She thanked him, then took a sip, but didn't relax until he took a few steps back and leaned against the edge of the desk.

"I'm Graydon Green," he said. "And I take it you're Rachel." He extended his hand toward her.

"Yes, Rachel Marconi." Warmth tingled where his rough palm rubbed against hers and she pulled away. "I really appreciate your help, Mr. Green."

"Please, call me Graydon. Do you need some ice for that?" He motioned to her hand.

She held it out in front of her. There was some redness around the knuckles and it still hurt a little, but she shook her head. "I've never hit anyone before. Not even my stupid brothers when they cut the hair off my Barbie dolls." She flexed her hand a few times, then transferred the water glass to it. The iciness felt good as it seeped into her hand.

"It looks like you did a decent job for your first try."

She twisted the glass around, listening to the clink of ice against glass. Calm, she repeated to herself. Find something else to focus on. She looked at the decor. "So, who's the hockey fan?"

His whole body tensed and became unnaturally still before relaxing. The moment passed so fast, she wasn't sure if she had really seen it or if it had been her imagination.

"The guys in my family. Any time we all get together, it's the only thing that can be on TV without someone complaining." He hesitated, then asked, "Do you like hockey?"

She shook her head. "Not really. But my dad and brothers follow almost everything—football, golf, soccer, bowling. I think I've interrupted them during a few hockey games. Personally, I think it's too violent." She looked again at all the hockey pictures, sure she had offended a die-hard fan. "Well, it's not just hockey. I feel the same way about football."

"Says the girl who just punched her boyfriend in the nose," Graydon said, a small lopsided smile made a dimple appear in one cheek.

Rachel snorted. "Believe me, he deserved it."

He remained silent, looking at her in a way that made her feel like he was weighing her comments. She met his gaze as they contemplated each other. Then she blurted out, "What is it with guys and lying?" He jolted in surprise. She continued before he could answer. "Seriously. Why do men think it's okay to cheat?"

Graydon held his hands out, as if defending himself from an ambush. "Just because I'm a guy doesn't mean I understand why others make the choices they do." He lowered his hands to grasp the edge of the desk. "To answer your question, I don't know. Maybe they grew up with dads who cheated or didn't have someone around to teach them the right way to treat a woman." He shrugged. "I do know there are lots of good guys out there."

"If there are, I haven't discovered proof of their existence."

He leaned slightly forward. "Is that what

tonight was about?"

Rachel turned her head away. She would never tell a stranger the truth. But how could she tell her family and best friend that she unwittingly became 'the other woman.' The one wives whisper about and plot revenge against. She gripped the glass of water, pondering how her life had taken this turn.

"My parents have been married for almost 40 years," she said. "These days, it seems like a miracle if a couple stays together long enough to celebrate their 10th anniversary." Their eyes met, hers moist while his were contemplative. "What happened that people don't love and respect each other through all the bumps anymore?"

The question sat in the silence of the room, dangling like a dead man at the end of a rope. Rachel's stomach tightened in a knot, creating a combination of queasiness and the urge to laugh at the horrendousness of the situation. She had gone from a startling, relationship-altering bomb being dropped to spewing her inner-most gut-wrenching questions about men and relationships to a total stranger.

She fidgeted in her seat, desperate to change the subject. Suddenly, it clicked in her mind who he reminded her of. "Has anyone ever said you look like that guy from The Pacifier?" His forehead scrunched in confusion. That should have been her clue to stop, but instead verbal diarrhea took over. "You know, the movie about the military guy who ends up babysitting. I'm terrible at remembering celebrities." She rubbed her forehead, trying hard to come up with the name that seemed to be on the edge of her memory. Anything to keep her mind distracted from tonight's disaster.

He cleared his throat. "You mean Vin Diesel?"

Her head snapped up. "That's it!"

"You think I look like Vin Diesel?"

"Yes! Well, other than you actually have hair and I guess he's on the short side and you're rather tall," she tilted her head, not able to stop the rambling. "But your faces are similar and you're both freakishly muscular—um, I mean . . ." Heat flooded her cheeks. His lips were thin and his eyes crinkled at the corners while mirth danced in the brown depths. "I'm sorry. I tend to put my foot in my mouth, or let it out as the case may be, but—" She didn't even finish the sentence before he began to laugh. Great. Where was the duct tape when you needed it?

A light knock caught her attention. She

turned to see the restaurant host standing at the door. "Your cab has arrived, miss."

Escape. The emergency exit she so desperately needed finally appeared. She gathered her things, then stood and bumped into Graydon.

"I'm sorry," she mumbled, hurrying out of the room.

"Wait." He followed her down the hall. She almost made it to the front entrance without speaking to him again. "Here, let me get the door for you." He reached around her and grabbed the handle.

Sure, anything to get me out of here faster. She brushed past him to the cab waiting at the curb, but paused when she thought she saw Nico's car parked at the corner. Has he been waiting for me all this time? She squinted to see if it really was him, but the car was parked in a poorly lit area of the street. The evening's darkness made it difficult to tell if someone sat inside or not.

Once more, Graydon materialized, this time to open the cab door. She wanted to slide in and escape, instead she turned toward him one last time. His expression was calm and warm. Chocolate. His eyes reminded her of melted chocolate just before mixing it into ganache. She blinked, then refocused. For a brief moment, gratitude pushed her desperation and anger aside.

"Thank you for helping me earlier." She started to move, but he took her hand and helped her into the cab, then briefly squeezed it before he stepped back.

"I hope you come back soon, Rachel Marconi." He closed the door and waved the driver on.

She turned in her seat. Graydon stood at the curb, hands in his pockets, watching her ride away. She faced forward and sighed. The night flashed through her mind like a bad movie rerun.

Well, one thing's certain. I'm an idiot. She wiped at the tears falling down her cheeks, pulled her cell out of her purse and hit speed dial. But at least I'm an idiot who has Ben & Jerry's and a best friend to share it with.

LOVE UNDER CONSTRUCTION

Charlee was angry . . .

What do you do when your boss makes someone else the lead on a big renovation project that should rightfully be yours? You quit. On second thought, that might not be the best idea, but Charlee Jackson has never been one for second thoughts. Instead, she lands a big contract of her own. She's jumping into her new life—work boots, tool belt and all. Now she just needs to form a company and hire contractors and buy supplies and get an office . . . and not fall in love with her former boss's son. Yeah. Definitely not that last one.

Peter was torn . . .

You can't date someone who works for you, but now that his dad let Charlee walk out the door, Peter Elliot is considering his options. Charlee was their top renovation expert, his best friend's sister, and the only thing that made the drudgery of running a large construction business bearable. But how do you date a competitor, especially one your father is trying to drive out of business? It would be stupid to make your dad angry right before he retires and hands the company over to you. Right?

When Charlee and Peter are scheduled to work on the same Indulgence Row house, their feelings and priorities are put to the test. They need to make a choice, and they better be quick about it, because the whole mixture is curing fast and threatening to crumble to pieces.

LOVE UNDER CONSTRUCTION

CHAPTER ONE PREVIEW

THE CLINK OF CHINA and chatter of women filled the room at City Hall where the Women in Business' monthly meeting was well under way. The typically boring room had been transformed. The plain brown tables and chairs for committee discussions were replaced with round tables covered with pretty white table clothes and seasonal centerpiece decorations. Elegant flower arrangements graced the podium as well as the sign-in table. Today's decor theme included glass bowls filled with pretty white and blue frosted balls. A few snowmen were positioned around the outside of the bowl, each holding a little banner with January written in a swirly font.

While most of the ladies appreciated the ambience, what really kept them coming back month after month was the best part — the food. If there was one good thing about the Women in Business group, they didn't scrimp on salads and dainty foods that barely made a dent in your stomach. Nope, they served good-sized portions and incredible desserts. After all, the group was all about making connections and serving the community—and what better way to do that than chatting over a delicious meal?

Charlee Jackson shifted out of the way so the servers could clear the table, all while following her friend Rachel's conversation as she gushed about her new fiancé.

"Graydon's the first guy I've met who's actually interested in conversation that isn't all about sports, which is shocking considering he was a hockey player," Rachel said, pushing her auburn hair back over her shoulder. The sparkle from the princess cut rock on her finger practically blinded anyone looking directly at it.

The only thing marring the picture of perfection was Rachel's bruised arm confined to a sling and her broken leg, which meant she was wheelchair bound for the next few weeks. Charlee admired Rachel's positive outlook, especially after being attacked at her last cake design competition.

"Are you sure he's not gay?" Charlee asked playfully.

Kristen, Rachel's business partner and

best friend, leaned close and confessed in a whisper. "Oh my gosh. I've caught them making out more than once, and all I can say is steam, baby," she said, fanning herself.

Poor Rachel's face flushed pink as she nudged Kristen with her elbow. "TMI, Kristen."

Charlee laughed. "Have you set a wedding date yet?"

"We're looking for a date in May," Rachel said. "I know it's only a few months away, but I'm pretty old-fashioned and I told Graydon I wasn't moving in with him until after we say I do."

"Ooh, that reminds me," Kristen said, leaning in. "Charlee, mark your calendar for the first Saturday in March. I'm planning the bridal shower. We're having a traditional get together with the parents, grandparents, and everyone, then something a little more fun for the evening with the younger ladies."

Before Rachel could reply, Marla Belliston called the monthly meeting to order from her coveted spot at the podium. As usual, Marla was dressed in a perfectly buttoned up, classy suit with her dark hair pulled up in an elegant twist. Charlee fidgeted in her seat, tucked a few pale blonde strands of her short A-line bob behind her ear, then folded her jean-clad legs to hide her work boots under the table. Not everyone could afford the business suits Marla wore and, honestly, working at a desk as an accountant wasn't Charlee's idea of fun anyway. Restoring and renovating houses— now that was her idea of perfection. Taking the old, updating it while keeping the charm of the original structure—pure happiness.

Still, a girl occasionally envies the whole put together feminine look.

"Before we continue to our program on community literacy by our wonderful librarian, Eden Tate, there are a few announcements from our secretary, Victoria Lyons."

Ah yes, another well put-together woman, although not nearly as formal and uppity as Marla. Victoria was actually quite nice and relatable, which was good since she was a Realtor and worked with a variety of people. She often called Charlee when she had clients who needed help getting homes on the market or a buyer who wanted to consult on renovations before submitting an offer. Victoria was smart, savvy, and sassy— a combination that made her not just a good business contact, but a fun friend, too.

Victoria took her place at the podium, dressed in dark pants and a French blue button-down blouse. Trendy, but casual.

Her deep red hair was pulled back in a sleek, low pony tail. "Ladies, it's time to begin preparations for our annual Autism fundraiser. The committee bantered around several ideas. Generally, we do a charity concert, a dinner and auction, or a golf tournament."

Charlee yawned. It seemed like the same choices every year. They'd raise the money they set as a goal, which was great, but still, boring.

"This year though," Victoria paused, waiting for the chatty members to turn their attention to the impending announcement. "The committee has come up with a twist on the auction theme. Instead of having items and services donated, we are planning a bachelor's auction."

Charlee sat up a little straighter. Now this could be interesting. From the gasps and oohs in the room, the rest of the club was eager, too.

Victoria continued. "The committee is still working out the details, but the bachelor's auction will be six months from now, in June. We need suggestions and contact information for your favorite single men. There's a box at the back of the room with slips of paper and pens next to it or you can email me after today's meeting."

Several women turned and eyed the box. Charlee could just imagine the wheels turning in their heads, plotting how to get there first and who to nominate for the auction block. They may as well skip the next twenty-five minutes dedicated to community literacy because the women's attention definitely wasn't on anything other than their top ten local hot guys list.

Victoria ran through a few additional business items, which Charlee mostly tuned out while she enjoyed her cheesecake drizzled with fudge sauce.

"I have one last announcement. Crystal Creek City Council has given approval to go ahead with a new shopping district. A private investor has purchased the homes along Taylor Avenue in Crystal Creek."

That was Charlee's grandmother's neighborhood. Or at least it was before Grandma passed away. Her house had sold at auction last year. Most of the other homes in that area had been sold as well. It was sad to see it go from the neighborhood of her youth, filled with laughter and fun, to what it was now—run down and mostly vacant. Even sadder still was the thought of everything being torn down to make a new shopping district. She set her cheesecake aside to pay better attention to Victoria.

"This new shopping district will be unique. The homes will remain intact, although they will be brought up to current code standards and also renovated inside for whichever businesses decide to relocate there. Not only will the neighborhood charm remain, but the investor's vision is for the shopping to be targeted to women and each store must be local and self-owned. No chains or franchises. The tentative name for the project is Indulgence Row. If you or someone you know might be interested in more information, please contact me. Thank you."

The other women may have been occupied with making a list of bachelors, but for the remainder of the meeting, all Charlee could think about was the Indulgence Row project.

She wondered who the investor was, because he certainly had great vision. The more she thought about the renovations and revitalizing the neighborhood, the more excited she became.

She wanted in.

She wanted to use her talents to bring her Grandmother's home—and all her former friends' homes around it—back to something filled with joy and people. The thought of people creating memories there again made her heart sing.

She would be a part of it.

After the meeting came the expected mad dash to the bachelor nomination box. But Charlee headed in the opposite direction toward Victoria, with Kristen wheeling Rachel close behind her. Eden Tate, the librarian who presented, also joined them at the table.

"Tell me more about Indulgence Row," Eden said, as she took the chair next to Victoria.

Charlee was glad to see Eden join them. She really liked the spunky woman, who was nothing like any of the other women who worked at the Crystal Creek library. Not that there was anything wrong with the sweet, gentle, and mostly gray-haired ladies, but Eden's spunky, modern and outgoing personality brought a whole new energy to the place.

Victoria talked a little more about the shopping district, feeling each of them out on their interest levels. "Each house will be renovated to fit the business that wants to occupy the space. Do you have someone in mind, Eden?"

"I'm actually quite interested," she replied.

"Oh!" Victoria said. "I didn't realize you

were leaving the library."

"There have been so many programs I've wanted to start, but with budget restrictions and different point of views about future readers, it's been difficult to implement them. I've been considering opening a bookstore for a while. Something charming and cozy, where readers can talk books, plots and even debate which couples from series are better than others." Eden continued, her excitement and enthusiasm showing through the expressive ways she moved her arms and hands as she shared her vision. "There's so much I want to do, to inspire a love of reading, host book clubs, hold genre spotlight nights, and oh so much more. I've been squirreling away bits of money here and there over the years. Once you mentioned Indulgence Row, I knew it was perfect for my shop."

"Me, too," Rachel chimed in. "Kristen and I have already talked to you about needing a new space. Our teeny tiny shop hasn't been able to handle the influx of customers we've had since the cake challenge. I can just see the quaint sign hanging from the front of the house. Sweet Confections," she said, with her hands raised as if framing an imaginary sign.

"Sweet Confections at Indulgence Row,"

Charlee chimed in. "That could be part of the branding. Each shop has its name, but followed with 'at Indulgence Row'."

"I love it," replied Victoria, jotting notes in her notepad.

"I totally want in," Charlee said, leaning forward. "I want to get together to talk specifics and have Elliott Construction put together a bid."

Victoria put her arm around Eden. "You all have brightened up my day. I'll contact the investor, then set up a time to meet with each of you. This is going to be an amazing project."

It will indeed, Charlee thought. Now, she just needed to get her boss on board.

*****

RATHER THAN RETURN to her job site at the Johnson's house, Charlee headed over to Elliott Construction's main office. All the way there, her feet tingled. Odd as it might sound, she knew better than to ignore her feet. The buzzing bee feeling was a sure sign that she was onto something great.

She had many wonderful memories of spending time with her grandparents when she was young. Then Pappy died and the only time she saw Grandma smile was when she was surrounded by her grandchildren. They gardened together, tending flower beds around the house and a veggie garden in the back yard. They baked cookies and Grandma taught her how to make homemade chicken noodle soup with delicious matzo balls. A craving came over Charlee to go home and make her favorite soup and continue reminiscing.

Instead, she got out of her truck and fought the bitter January wind to enter the office building. She would convince George Elliott that this project was perfect for them. Not only for the company, but for her first lead project.

She had been working for the company since she was sixteen years old. She started out in the offices until she proved to George that she was just as handy with a hammer as his son, Peter. Not only handy, but she had a great sense for space and design, and could envision in her head what needed to happen to achieve the finished product the client desired. After a two year leave to get a dual degree in carpentry and home remodeling and preservation, she resumed her work with Elliott Construction, where it all began.

In all these years, she had yet to be the crew lead for her own project.

But this one she would. She would make sure of it.

Charlee knocked on the wood door frame of George's office. He was seated at his desk, busy with a phone call, but waved her in. His salt and pepper head bent over a yellow legal pad as he scrawled notes across the page.

"That all sounds good, Randy. Let me know when the supplies are delivered. Thanks." George replaced the phone in the cradle and made a few notes before turning his attention to her. "What can I do for you, Charlee?"

"I just got back from the Women in Business meeting," she said, sitting down in the hard, cracked chair in front of his cluttered desk.

"Oh, right. That was today, wasn't it?" He pushed up the sleeves of his flannel shirt, then started sorting through the mail piled on his desk.

"Victoria Lyons announced a new shopping district." That got George's attention, his eyes finally meeting hers. "You know the area where my grandparents lived?"

He nodded in acknowledgement. "Sure, I used to go down there for card games with your grandfather."

"They plan to renovate those blocks of homes into a shopping district. Not new construction, but actually restoring the houses themselves and renovating them to fit the businesses that will be there."

His face brightened. "That sounds great. Thanks, Charlee. I'll have Peter talk to Victoria and get a bid in."

She shook her head and tried not to fidget. Would he go for her plan? "I already talked with her. George, I want to lead the project."

He sat back in his chair, steepled his hands in front of his chest and sighed. "Peter has more experience in this area. He's done city bids before, he knows the ins and outs—"

"Only because you haven't let me," she interrupted. "Peter may have more years with the company, but I have more education. You know I've helped Peter with building plans and offered a lot of good suggestions for better techniques and plan improvements. Things he didn't know about because he didn't go to college and take—"

George's fist came down hard on his desk. "This job isn't about a college degree and just because you have one, doesn't make you more qualified."

She should have known better than to

bring up her education. It had been a constant sore point between them. Instead she changed her tactics and continued with a calm tone. "George, I really want to lead this. I'm connected to it. Please, I'm ready. You know I am."

There was a moment of silence before he replied. "Peter will lead the project. You can have your pick of crew to work on, but he will be in charge. Maybe next time." George returned to sorting his mail. When she didn't move to leave, he glanced up, "Aren't you supposed to be working on the Johnson's place?"

Instead, Charlee leaned forward. He was never going to change his attitude. It was time to make her stand. "You put me on the most expensive projects. Why is that?"

Startled, George returned his attention to her. His eyes narrowed, making the wrinkles around them bunch up like craggy rocks. When he remained silent, she forged ahead. "You know it's because I'm damn good. The best renovator you have on staff."

"Maybe," he replied curtly, trying his best to not give her any extra ground to prove her point.

She shook her head. "There's no maybe about it. If you don't let me take the lead, then I'll give notice."

His eyes widened briefly, before narrowing into slits again. "You wouldn't."

Charlee simply crossed her arms and met his gaze, not wavering.

"You can sit there, stubborn, as long as you want. I'm not budging either." He folded his hands on the desk, his face a cool, calm facade. His famous poker face.

But this time, he wasn't going to win. She had been sitting in the proverbial back seat, waiting for him to wake up and smell the coffee. During her last semester of college, she was a lead contractor for the construction company she interned for. She had been willing to step back a few notches when she returned home, assuming George would eventually get over the fact that she was a woman working in a 'man's job'.

It had been six years of telling herself to be patient, but she was done. Her tingling feet told her that Indulgence Row wasn't just a project—it was her project.

Charlee uncrossed her legs and stood, not once breaking eye contact. "Then I guess it's settled. Consider this my notice. I'll finish the Johnson project, then clear out." She pivoted away and walked to the door.

George's chair scraped against the hardwood floors. His voice boomed through the room. "You will not! Charlee," he warned, his voice menacing. "Don't be a stubborn fool."

She turned the knob, then paused before opening it. "There's only one stubborn fool in this room." She opened the door, then stepped out, closing it behind her.

His voice boomed through the door. "Charlee, get the hell back in here!"

Instead, she walked past the wide-eyed receptionist and gawking co-workers who were finishing their lunch break. It wasn't unusual for their boss to yell, but Charlee ignoring the boss—that was definitely new.

Charlee pushed through the front door, out into the bright afternoon sun. She fisted her hand, hoping the bite of short nails into her palm would release the frustration crowding and bursting within. Hot dog! Did she just quit her job?

Breathe, girl, just breathe.

Grandma always said to never be afraid of change because it could lead to some of the best things in life.

I sure hope you're right, Grandma, cause I'm jumping in—work boots, tool belt, and all.

Acknowledgements

A big round of applause goes to . . .
drum roll, please

Tamara Heiner, my amazing editing chick. Thank you for helping me to have confidence in developing my very first novella!

Steven Novak, cover designer extraordinaire.

Lisa Swinton, my European adventure brainstorming chick. Thanks for joining me on this journey!

Heather Justesen, who has instant download access to at least half of my writer's brain. So glad you keep it safe for whenever I feel lost.

My awesome review team. *waves madly from recliner*

The munchkins. We may not live in Oz, but you are cute and adorable, no matter how old you are! *big squishy hugs*

Mr. Ferguson. One day, I'll take you to La Rochelle & be your personal tour guide. Love you more! xoxoxo

ABOUT THE AUTHOR

Danyelle Ferguson fell in love with La Rochelle, France as an exchange student her senior year of high school. Now she dreams about returning to share all her favorite places with her hubby.

Once Upon a Wish is her tenth published book. She's the award-winning author of the Indulgence Row series and several nonfiction books.

She is currently experiencing mountain-withdrawal while living in Kansas with her husband and four angels-in-training.

Website - www.DanyelleFerguson.com
Facebook- @AuthorDanyelleFerguson
Twitter - @DanyelleTweets